30 Under 30

an anthology of innovative
fiction by younger writers

Blake Butler &
Lily Hoang, eds.

Starcherone Books   Buffalo, NY

General Editor: Ted Pelton
Book Design: Rebecca Maslen
Proofreaders: Emmett Haq, Katharina Plucinski, & Jason
 Pontillo
Cover Design: Zach Dodson

30 under 30 : an anthology of innovative fiction by
younger writers / Blake Butler & Lily Hoang, eds.
     p. cm.
Includes bibliographical references.
ISBN 978-0-9842133-3-7 (pbk. : alk. paper)
 1. Youths' writings, American. 2. Experimental fiction,
American. 3. American fiction--21st century. I. Butler,
Blake. II. Hoang, Lily K. III. Title: Thirty under thirty.
 PS647.Y68A15 2011
 813'.010806--dc23

2011019019

State of the Arts

NYSCA

Starcherone Books, Inc., is supported by
taxpayers of the state of New York, through
the New York State Council for the Arts, a
state agency.

Starcherone Books, Inc., a 501(c)(3) nonprofit, also thanks
the many individuals and private entities who have made
contributions to this literary educational organization, in
the furtherance of our nonprofit mission.

TABLE OF CONTENTS

JOANNA RUOCCO
FROG

The blue paint of the broken wing soaks up the sun and that's where Charlotte and I curl up at night, sharing the warmth.

"It's sort of like spooning," says Charlotte. I don't say anything. Overhead, the vast, black sky. Orion's belt, but vertical. Orion's button-fly. One, two, three stars. The sky is closed tight against us.

"Because spoons are metal?" says Charlotte. She taps my shoulder.

"You know?" she says.

* * *

The first thing I saw, a man, face down on the little beach, with his legs in the water. He had a hairy neck and was wearing a T-shirt that said "NO MA'AM" on the back, a vertical column of red letters. I stepped closer and saw that the each red letter started a new word. The shirt really said: National Organization of Men Against Amazonian Masterhood.

"Are you dead?" I called. The man looked all in one piece, but his face was planted squarely in the sand. Breathing would not be advisable in that circumstance. Most likely his heart had stopped when we came through the cumulonimbus. My heart almost stopped then, too. All the static and wind.

"Hi, Justine," said a voice, which was much louder than my voice. Her voice had always been much louder than my voice. In case I had neck trauma, I decided not to turn and look at her. I sighed.

"Hi Charlotte," I said.

* * *

A long time ago, when jet travel started, stewardesses came through the aisles and gave you frosty glass bottles of coca-cola and root beer, those heavy greenish ones. I think they're antiques. Now you just get cans, mini-cans, not even twelve ounces. You can't put a message in a mini-can. Charlotte tried. She found a paperback thriller and let it dry on top of some coral. We didn't have any pens so she went through the wrinkled pages and ripped out relevant words.

"They're going to have to arrange them so it makes sense," said Charlotte. She was slipping the little scraps through the pop-top.

"Look," she said. "I found a 'Charlotte!' " She put the can in the ocean and we watched it move up and down, in the same place, like a buoy.

"It's not going anywhere," I said.

"Give it time," said Charlotte. She sat down cross-legged, facing the other direction.

* * *

For a while there was just white sand, blue water, and small items of wreckage. Then the sea sort of roiled, and the middle portion of the jet surfaced in a font of bubbles, the bubbles rising intact into the air. A small, gasoline-smelling swell lapped over our legs. We leapt up, back to back, like when outlaws find themselves surrounded. It's hopeless, but they prepare to fight anyway, watching enemies close in around them from all directions. We stood just like that, except that the outlaws are usually partners, brothers or lovers. The contempt they feel for society is nothing next to the love they feel for each other, and when they put their backs together they're saying, "I will protect you with my body. I will take the bullets in my breast. I will die for you and you will die for me. In that way, my death becomes a gift. Something beautiful."

Being on a desert island should be like that. A covenant. Potent doom. Lots of fucking. I watched the jet breech, roll over in the water, hissing and booming, spray and foam falling all around. I felt Charlotte's wing bones and mine, grating together.

"I'm going to move now, Charlotte," I said. "Don't fall down." I took a step forward and her body came with me, arcing.

* * *

"Hello, this is Diana Paloma of Women in Business, and I'm here tonight with Justine, creator of Inflatable

Justine. Justine, how did you come up with the idea for Inflatable Justine?"

"Well..."

"You patented Inflatable Justine shortly after your rescue from a remote Pacific island where, if I understand correctly, you landed virtually unscathed by a thirty-thousand foot drop from the cabin of a criminally under-maintained commercial jet, operated by a company which has since collapsed."

"Yes, I..."

"Did that experience prompt your development of Inflatable Justine, whose enormous success has revolutionized emergency response technology while simultaneously shattering the safety-glass ceiling for Women in Business? Do you hold any rancor towards Luther Murks, president of Night Flight, the company whose criminal negligence resulted in the deaths of 257 passengers and crewmembers and your own harrowing seventh-month ordeal? Do you agree with speculations that Luther Murks is, in fact, an alias for Luther Lux, leader of Death Deluxe, a doomsday cult linked to several domestic and international incidents and currently under investigation by US intelligence? Are you concerned by the unknown whereabouts of Luther Murks? Do you feel that the notoriety of the Night Flight trials has positively impacted your sales? How will your product outlast the publicity? What are your future dreams and do they include new lines of Inflatable Justines? What about Inflatable Justines of different ages, races, genders? Do you agree with accusations that Inflatable Justine reinforces certain culturally-specific beliefs about beauty that are, in fact, white supremacist? In your mind, does the practical life-giving capacity of Inflatable Justine and your personal success as a Woman in Business cancel out the harm done by your perpetuation of stereotypes regarding woman as passive, as "receivers," if you will, the doormat re-envisioned as safety net? Is Inflatable Justine in the missionary position? Should she be used in the rescue of children under the age of eighteen?"

* * *

You are driving past a nursing home fire. The road is blocked with fire trucks. Firemen are running through the lobby doors, laying the old people on the grass. The old people lie very still, getting chemical burns from the lawn, which is intensely green. The fireman race in and out of the nursing home, but many more old people are still trapped inside. Ladies in flouncy, floral-print polyester-rayon blend nightgowns scream to you from Constant Care.

"Help," they scream. "Fire!" Their acrylic knitting projects are like incendiary bombs, igniting all around them. The strong ones lift the wheelchairs of the weak. They tip the chairs, struggle to dump the bundled figures. For a moment, between the burning curtains, you glimpse the tiny faces, purple hair glowing like sterno, white, waving hands. Bodies drop from the ledges.

Breathe. Position your Inflatable Justine on the sidewalk. The nursing home is fourteen-stories. The sky fills with floral-patterned smoke. Gray hydrangeas.

Steely widows from Independent Living are rescuing their heirlooms. They're throwing commemorative plates and jewelry boxes. Fake pearls rain down on Inflatable Justine. Constant Care ladies fall with their legs bent, like they're still in wheelchairs, and Inflatable Justine takes the impact, flattens slightly, and refills, her breasts rising. The women bounce gently, knees drawn up. Falling, they were weightless. Their joints did not hurt. They felt the air on their faces like when they rode in cars, very fast, with the windows down through the mountains, or maybe they sailed in ships, or jumped horses, or just strolled on the boardwalk with two good legs. It seemed to them, falling, like they were already dead. They were souls. They had been released into the night. They saw Inflatable Justine, waiting, far below, and as they hurtled towards her, they imagined they were returning to the bodies of their youth. That's why their hearts never failed, falling. Their hearts beat strongly, for joy. Cardiac arrest kills people who fall from great heights more often than the ground does. This is a matter of time, of relative distance. The ground is so far away and your heart is so close.

* * *

The first week we did not hear any noises, see any changes other than a lightening and darkening of the hazy blue. My eyes began to pick out strange patterns in the sand grains and the tiny white breaks of the waves. Weird, branching shapes. I had a boyfriend. He told me if you go long enough with no external stimulation, your brain reverses the direction of its signals. The optic nerve transmits backwards. You can start to see the fibers inside your head, neurons and dendrites, pulses of electricity, blood. I liked this boyfriend. He was smart. We drove to the Adirondacks and fucked rustically, in a tent. I'd never fucked in a tent before. My spine against a rock. It smelled like raincoats. We walked to a murky pond, and he scooped a handful of brown water, and showed me the black tadpoles wiggling in his fingers.

"The light makes the shape of a frog," he told me. "All the particles of the universe contain their full potential. Everything is vibrating towards perfection."

Sometimes, I'd catch him squinting down at me. I knew he had glimpsed it, then, my completed being. He needed to shield his eyes against the radiance.

I squinted at Charlotte in the dark and tried to read her future in the blur. I couldn't really tell anything from the smudges. She could be inside a subway, in some safe, clean city. Or the darkness might be digestive. The two us eaten up by sharks or squids, extruded in an underwater cloud. The two of us, storm systems on the ocean floor.

Pinging www.l.scopuli.com [18.1.8A.9: 22 miles south
of the Southwest most point of the last and least bit-
ten part, the first resting spot of the New Jersey dead
before returning to the cemetery behind the soccer
fields behind the baseball fields behind your house, the
house that I would arrive at, but never enter, a house
where my name was spoken to mothers and grand-
mothers still dusting off late antiquity from wedding
dresses elsewhere, L on the map, if the map included
your mother, a woman of lines and earrings, a woman
who loved me without meeting me, no doubt due to
your annotations of myself: oh yes, most definitely,
he knows what he's doing and where he's going; he
knows languages that no one else knows or pretends
to know and with this language he creates addresses
which host addresses, a pir8 map with words that
change color when you touch them, you really should
meet him, no he doesn't know the words to Mazurek

Dabrowskiego. It is fitting that we shared White Russians in neon, my hand underneath the glass, lifting it up to your, smiling at me with your. But you, harborer of mills and fuel and food stations named after infantry with infantile poetics, harborer of harbors, arbors, ships, shit and love for men in other countries, fighting wars from and for birds, giving me digital handshakes, checkboxes that signify that I agree to these terms, you must agree to these terms if you want to continue functioning, despite wanting to show him what nothing can do to a man like me ((the answer is something to you)), you, harborer, forgo the encryption, the WEP, the cavalcade of alternating capital and lowercase letters and insignificant numbers and give yourself permission to alter system files and documents, media files of numbers meant to signify an organ, numbers representing a color representing a patch of blonde hair (((I see you in squares)), pointless applications and Other. Read Only.] with 22 bytes of data:

Reply from 18.1.8A.9: bytes=32 time=23ms TTL=245
Reply from 18.1.8A.9: bytes=32 time=22ms TTL=245
Reply from 18.1.8A.9: bytes=32 time=25ms TTL=246
Reply from 18.1.8A.9: bytes=32 time=22ms TTL=246

Ping statistics for 18.1.8A.9:
Packets: Sent [202.22.78.523 (22 miles from ?, an amalgamation of fields, trees, roads, reservoirs, and hills that are unincorporated: a place created solely

for statistical purposes and the tabulation of zip codes. To diagnose the place of my upbringing and upgrading from ghost to server would involve handshakes and the divvying up of hot air balloons; the splitting of claims to the kidnapped children of aviators and the innocents with blood-laced ladders. So we, and by extension, me, are autonomous regions; islands surrounded by land infested with hammerheads and coral. The self that knows itself as a particle of nothing larger is launched against jet streams to recognized places with recognizable people with no pins to snap into place; no room for expansion. We the people of the autonomous region of Readington Township, named after a porticoed powerlodge where past kings boxed up bear cubs in cages on lawns under Maryland/Virginia annex moons, slurping alkaline to be used in rice wine to be used for batteries and where future kings will discuss liberation theories, are zipped and archived easily; an apathetic mudslide, a deluge, soaking and sticking myself to other nothings, dust, dirt, static in the line, in hopes of bringing us somewhere, elsewhere. The numbers and origins match; I shout from the top of the dam of the reservoir that keeps water from crashing through windows, fish swimming through convex monitors, and myself from being electrocuted. It keeps us from being complacently washed over, algae joining us together, submerged. But this is the only way how; to set type and code to zero, to host and to route to and through.)]= 4 Received = 4, Lost = 4 (100% loss, there is no echo),

Approximate round trip times in milli-seconds:

Minimum = 22ms, Maximum = 25ms, Average = 23ms nowhere is somewhere, at least the in grand scheme of things, and believe you me, I am from a somewhere where the grand scheme of things is some-where we want to be. Between you and me, there is not much going on between.

There is nothing between us but interchanges, gaps to jump, the need to swing from cable to cable. When you are above the ground, there is no meeting half-way, dangling like a peripheral cord. We pool together elsewhere, state capitals where we can take trains to Southern states where we can share vegetables and cake instead of alcohol and milk, eastern cities on the water where they used to crown pageant queens be-fore they got in boats with older lovers and circled the shoreline, places where we are both slave and host. But as long as A is a place that exists, founded by IP addresses fragmented by points and the old guard with gravel in bone, a CAT5 carrying sandy families with gritty ice cream cones from home to water and back, workers from split-levels to parking lots, and you, presumably from blood duck soup to Route 9. You never allowed me to pass; bandwidth bottlenecked af-ter failed proposals and attempts to widen pathways: to allow bits through.

MICHAEL J. LEE
LAST SEEN

A mother and her son sit at their kitchen table. They are ruined people, both in appearance and spirit.

There was, and still might be, a brother to the son, a son to the mother. Who disappeared from their lives not long ago. He took the dog for a walk one bright Saturday and never came back.

We sympathize. We really do. So would he. Pity is easy for us; it's empathy that we find difficult. But we'll give it a try. We give all people one or two or possibly three chances.

It's late afternoon. The light is ugly and yellow and violating the darkness of the kitchen as it streams through the blinds. At least that's the mother's opinion. Everything has become awful to her; the light, the dark, the modest house in which they live, the people they encounter on a daily basis. Except of course her son, whom she loves. The son has not yet reached his mother's stage of evacuation. But, to be fair, he does have some hateful seedling already growing in his heart.

The son is only nine, but has the face of an old man. It has been a difficult three months. The days have passed slowly. The son doesn't know this yet, but he will have to learn to live with his face. He believes he will shed it in adulthood. He is so sweet and wrong.

They, the mother and son, channel different frequencies of pain. Neither knows exactly what the other is feeling. This is a condition invented long ago by a pervert. To each his own private horror, the pervert says. Grief will be unending and barely endurable. Lay all your troubles on you know who.

It seems unrealistic that one family should suffer so much, we think. Awful statistics, we say. Random accidents. (A plan, he says. A developing plan.)

There are some woods near the house, a square mile at the end of the street. Bring on the deforested future, we say. Less places to get lost. What is a child's safety to a little lost wood?

The son has a notebook, on which he's written the facts of the case. He doesn't fully understand what he's written. He just writes what he hears, what he reads or sees on television. His mother stares blankly, angrily at the window and the light seeping through it.

I want to look for him, says the son.

Why? says the mother.

We've let other people look for us.

They have been over this many times. The son still believes that his brother can be found.

Why don't we look for him?

Where would we look?

The woods, says the son.

We've looked in the woods.

Somewhere else then.

The world is too large.

Why do you want to forget him?

I can't forget him.

The mother is right, of course. Oh, that we could forget everything, we say.

Why don't you care? says the son.

But I do, says the mother. I'm trying to accept his absence. I hope you can too.

But he's not gone. He's missing.

Really? Do you really believe that?

Come look for him with me, says the son.

The mother turns her face toward him. Her expression is haggard, furious. Think for a moment, she says. What do we know?

About what?

What are the facts?

Why? says the son. He looks at his mother with his poor hopeful face.

I'll help you if you answer me, she says.

Ok.

Where was he last seen?

He was last seen at the trail head.

By whom?

He was last seen by an elderly couple at the trail head.

Our neighbors. Who are decrepit cunts.

Why would you call them that?

Tell me what they saw.

They saw him talking to a gray-haired man in a gray truck.

And?

They took down the license plate of the gray truck and walked away.

Decrepit cunts.

Why would you call them that?

A decrepit cunt has a keen sense of danger but not the courage to locate the source of the danger, for they are too decrepit. Hence the taking down of the license plate without actually intervening.

So he was last seen by our neighbors, an elderly couple, who are a pair of decrepit cunts.

Yes. Read me what else you have.

Our dog was found in the woods, walking alone without a leash.

And what did we do with the dog?

We had it put to sleep.

And why did we do that?

Because it was an unbearable reminder of my brother.

Yes. What else do you have there?

The police were able to find the truck, because of our neighbors.

What did they find in the truck?

They found two things, says the son.

Which were?

They found a dog leash.

And whose dog did it belong to?

Ours.

And where is our dog?

In the ground.

Good. What else did they find?

They found something that wasn't there.

What was it?

They found that the seatbelt had been cut out.

Good. And what did police find in the dumpster behind the super market?

They found the missing seatbelt.

And what was special about the seatbelt?

It was bloody.

Did it match your brother's blood type?

Yes.

How does this make you feel?

Scared. How does it make you feel?

Angry.

Why not scared?

I'm not scared of anything. What did the police not find?

The gray-haired man and my brother.

And why haven't they found your brother?

Because the haven't found the gray haired man.

And why haven't they found the gray haired man?

Because the police are limited?

Yes. Any other reason?

Because the gray-haired man is wily.

Yes. How does this make you feel?

Angry. Stop asking me questions.

Why?

You're making me scared.

Ok.

Do you remember your sister?

Yes.

What happened to her?

She was killed by a car.

And what happened to the perpetrator?

He went to jail.

Do you remember your father?

Yes.

And what happened to him?

He died of cancer.

And what happened to the cancer?

It died with him.

Good. Do you see how these things happen?

Yes.

Do you believe your brother is dead?

No.

Why not?

Because he is still missing.

But the facts.

I know.

Do you believe that the gray-haired man is guilty?

Yes.

And what has happened to him?

Nothing.

What do we need to do?

Find my brother.

No, says the mother. What do we need to do?

I don't know.

Who do we need to find?

The gray-haired man.

Yes. Why?

I don't know.

Will he bring your brother back?

No.

Why do we need to find the gray-haired man?

Because he can tell us what he knows.

Good. But will what he knows bring your brother back?

No.

Why?

Because my brother is probably dead.

Good. Then why would we care to listen to the gray haired man?

I don't know.

Because the gray-haired man will have interesting things to say.

Since when do we care about hearing interesting things?

We are starting today.

I don't want to.

Do we have anything else to look forward to?

Why do you keep reminding me that my brother is dead?

Because grief has made me strange.

Me too.

I'm sorry.

Are you making an excuse?

Yes. Is it a good one?

Yes.

She takes her son's head in her hands and kisses him. Do you know why I love you?

Because I'm your last one?

No.

Why then?

Because you will never die.

I hope so.

Do you still want to look for your brother?

Yes.

Get your coat, then.

We might have made a mistake. The world is too big and full of life to dwell here, we think. Broad parody, we shout. They don't resemble anyone we know. The mother? Sadism drives her. The son? Delusional, traumatized. Write him off. Write them both off, we say. In fact, write off the house, the neighborhood, the neighbors, the woods, the whole town, everyone is clearly complicit.

Here is a scene we would much prefer: a mother and her son sit at the breakfast table. The mother serves the son pancakes, the son eats them with gratitude. The son is getting ready for school, the mother talks to her son about the coming day. (Have compassion, he would say. Honor those beneath you with your attention. The mother is the very picture of endurance, the son innocent, incorruptible.) Fine, we say. Just get them out of the house, into the sunlight, the fresh air. Please just get them out of the house!

The mother and son begin to look. They leave the house, the mother closing the door behind them. Outside, autumn and its acute sadness. Piles of fallen leaves. The air is cold, beautiful to breathe in.

The mother takes her son's hand. They don't speak, making their way to the woods. This would be an appropriate time to pull away, we think. To be left with this image. Two wretched people strengthened only by each other. But we are feeling better outside.

We don't dare search their thoughts, yet we stay with them. Our own motivation escapes us, sometimes.

The mother and son are at the trail head now, looking. They enter the woods, the pine trees tall and teetering slightly in the wind. The son points to places off the trail, a hollow trunk, a branch, the dirty stream, and they search them all. They wind their way through the square mile, sometimes on the path, sometimes off, until both believe that they've exhausted every hiding place. When they reach the trail head the mother stops and squeezes her son's hand.

Are you satisfied? says the mother.

Yes, says the son.

Did you see the gray-haired man?
No. Did you?
Yes.
Where was he?
He was high up in a tree.
What was he doing?
Looking.
Did he see you?
Yes, says the mother.
What did he do?
He regarded me.
What did you do?
I regarded him.
Should we tell anyone?
No.
Why not?
He's not going to hurt us.
How do you know?
Because you can't hurt someone high in a tree.
Shouldn't he be punished?
I don't know.
Why didn't you tell me?
I didn't want you to be scared.
I wouldn't have been scared.
Do you want to see him now?
No, says the son. Did you see my brother?
No. Did you?
Yes.
Where was he?

He was high up in a tree.

Did he see you?

No.

I'm sorry. What was he doing?

I don't know.

Was he dead?

Yes.

Why didn't you tell me?

I didn't want you to be angry.

I wouldn't have been angry.

Do you want to see him now?

No.

Why not? says the son.

I remember him alive, says the mother.

Do you want to go home?

Yes.

Good.

We walk them to their door, but only out of courtesy. At last the sun has fallen, the putrid light bless-
edly gone. The neighborhood dark, the woods darker.
The mother and son deranged beyond help, the victim
and killer high up in trees! We've seen enough. We are
on the wrong side of town anyway. We have families to
return to, healthy children to care for. We've certainly
tried, and that is what matters. Will matter. (He will call
us weak-stomached, infantile, rational, graceless.) Let
him. Let him threaten us vaguely with eternity. There
are worse things. We don't believe him anyway. Let

them tell it themselves, we say:

good morning son good morning mother did you sleep well yes and you yes I made you some pancakes i would love some come sit down i will are you still satisfied yes are you yes do you know why i love you because i will live forever yes and because you are my last one will you live forever yes so will I do you miss the rest of them every one of them do you every one of them but we are getting along we are getting along will you answer the door yes hello sit down please sit down please we are listening yes we are listening what do you have to say please tell us what you have to say you dont need to explain or apologize just tell us what you have to say

.

ANGI BECKER STEVENS
BLOOD, NOT SAP

I was just getting ready for bed when the old oak tree in my backyard turned into a man. I didn't see it happen, there was just a loud cracking noise, like lightning splitting wood apart, and when I looked out the window to see what it was, the tree was gone and the man was there, walking toward my house. Normally, I wouldn't have opened my door for a strange man at night, but I felt like I knew him; he was my tree.

There was a gentle rain falling outside, and the man stood dripping in my kitchen. Everything about him was brown: brown hair, brown eyes, skin that was a human color but that made you think, instead, of the wood inside of a tree. You would think he would have been naked, but he was fully dressed: brown pants, a green button-down shirt, brown boots. He seemed clean, just damp, a different sort of damp than wet from the rain. He was musty. I expected him to seem disoriented in my house, but he seemed, more than anything, to be tired. There were questions I wanted to ask him, but I was tired, too, so I gave him a blanket and put him to bed on the living room couch. He was polite; he took off his boots and set them gently on the floor.

He took his coffee black. He showered upstairs, and afterwards he didn't smell any less like dirt and bark and leaves. It was okay; they weren't bad smells for a man. I asked him if he was the tree, or if he had been inside the tree, and he said he didn't exactly know. I asked him how long he had been the tree, or inside of the tree, and he didn't know that either. So we just sat side by side on my couch, watching the home and garden channel. When a carpenter fed some wood into a table saw, I looked at him guiltily. But he didn't flinch, at least not in any way that showed on the outside.

For the first few weeks, I missed the tree. I would look out across the yard when I stood at the sink rinsing dishes, and the place where the oak had stood seemed sad and empty. It was an old tree, a strong tree. Back when my husband was still around, I used to think that we would hang a tire swing in it someday. My husband wasn't built like a tree, but I could picture him running in circles, pushing a tire tied to a rope, with a little girl hanging on for dear life. I could picture how he would let go, and she would spin delirious circles through the air, thinking that she was going

to fly away, thinking that her daddy was as big and
strong as a tree. But my husband left before there ever
was a swing, or a little girl to ride it, and now I didn't
even have the tree.

Though of course, I did. He was so quiet that I
sometimes forgot he was there. I noticed mostly when
the coffee pot emptied twice as fast, and when I found
myself rinsing twice as many dishes. I hadn't really
minded living alone, but I hadn't really enjoyed it, either, the way some people do. The man who used to
be my tree was a kind of compromise between the
two, at least in the beginning: he was there, and not
there. I was alone, and not.

One night, we were sitting on my couch watching
David Letterman, and I reached out and touched his
wrist. He turned his arm over, I traced the path of his
veins with my fingertip. Blood? I asked. Or sap? He
shrugged, and smiled, a perfect grin. His teeth were
straight and white. I think blood, he said. And I told
him I thought so, too.

We started going out for walks together sometimes in the evenings. The man who used to be my
tree towered over me, not in a ridiculous or impossible way, but in a way that I wasn't used to. I had
never found myself attracted to that kind of man, the
large, the muscular, but there was something surpris-
ingly comforting about him, that made me think how

it would feel to be wrapped in his arms, and in the musty, woodsy, damp scent of him. We spent our walks mostly quiet, because there weren't many things he had to talk about. But sometimes we held hands. His skin wasn't rough like bark, it was smooth, like something newly born. Sometimes, sparrows would land for a few seconds on his shoulders. He always smiled, then: bashful, proud.

Who can say where people come from, what difference their history makes?

The first time we made love, it was like climbing a tree, going higher and higher into the leaves and branches until you're a part of the tree, until the damp, dirt smell is on your skin, too. The way you take it on some dumb, blind faith that the branches are going to support your weight, even though they get thinner the further you get from the ground.

When I wrap my hands around his biceps, I can't remember if I ever held on to the old oak tree this way, if I ever lifted my feet up and hung there, but I know that if I ever did, this is exactly what it would have felt like.

Sometimes, I worry that he will disappear as easily as he appeared, that he will harden into wood again. I touch his flesh when he sleeps, I check to make sure it is no less fleshy than ever. I put my hand on his chest as it rises and falls and I believe in blood, not sap. And I wonder if he was sliced clean through here if there would be rings one inside another, and if they would tell me anything I don't already know.

SHANE JONES
BLACK KIDS IN LEMON TREES

001: Looking over the edge of a cloud, I can see two people standing at opposite ends holding a giant banner. The banner reads: **ALL YOU COPS ARE IN THE CLOUDS**.

002: When we first found ourselves stuck in the clouds we just stood there in our uniforms, ready hands on guns. Someone said, we're stuck in the clouds. I looked around & counted 200 cops including myself. Including you, holding my lucky gun hand.

003: I remember being on the ground. I remember falling asleep. I remember telling you that we are more than uniforms. Then your cop hat blowing back. Then, in the clouds. Then, the overwhelming desire to pull my gun trigger, swing my club. Our handcuffs are the stitching between clouds.

004: I don't know what we're doing up here but down there buildings are on fire. When I lie down on a cloud to look over the edge, I feel the heat burning a hole through my stomach. My back is cold.

005: We shoot our guns wildly into the face of the sun. If a bird cuts through a cloud we beat it with our clubs. Our dark blue uniforms, the swinging of steel ringed clubs in the strange, cloud-high sunlight.

006: We don't know what we're doing up here when everything is going wrong down there. All us cops stuck in the clouds. Some jump off to try & save the world. Us others, we take turns shooting at each other from the far side of clouds. We hold hands & have evening orgies where we lick dicks & hips. An entire cloud filled with the tearing open of cop uniforms. All you see is naked limbs sticking up from cloud.

007: When it gets dark, the flames from the world below make the clouds glow orange. We take turns placing our guns in our mouth & pulling the triggers. Our cop heads explode across the night sky, our blood spots stars. Our uniforms become origami birds that can't fly because the corners of their wings are burning. In the morning, when we wake, our heads are back & attached. Our blue uniforms complete with badge & hat are clean & pressed.

008: Just look. Where. In the clouds. For what. All the cops are up there. We should save them. We need to harvest the lemons.

009: Sometimes a plane flies through the clouds & you can see the pilot making this big screaming face. A massive, **OH NO**. A few cops jump on the wings & leave us but they will be back in the morning crying into their hands.

010: A note appears on a cloud. The note says: **WE CAN HELP YOU IF YOU WILL BE GOOD**. All of us cops look at each other & don't know what to do. One cop punches the cloud. He's crying. Another note appears the next morning & the note says: **JUST LOOK DOWN & WE WILL WAVE**.

011: At one cloud when we look over the edge we can see a group of black kids waving. The black kids are crawling up & across the branches of lemon trees. There's a whole field of lemon trees & black children wearing neon pink shorts & nothing else.

012: How can they help us. I don't know. They did put those notes up here. Okay. Go ahead, drop a note.

013: Our note says: **YES WE WANT YOUR HELP** & it's written on a piece of cloud we saturate with our urine so it will fall into the lemon trees.

014: The worst group of people in the history of the world are cops who are lonely & have nothing to do. Our suicide rate is ridiculously high. When we shoot our throats open, lemons pour out. We wait for another note from the children.

015: The note says: **OKAY WE ARE GOING TO GET YOU DOWN FROM THOSE CLOUDS**.

016: Days pass. Weeks. We are tired of eating birds. The sun is blinding. The sun has faded our once dark blue uniforms into sky blue.

017: Another note appears. The note says: **HELLO. WE THOUGHT THE LEMON TREES WOULD GROW HIGHER & REACH YOUR CLOUDS BY NOW. WE APOLOGIZE. YOU'RE GOING TO HAVE TO JUMP**.

018: We scream down **HOW DO YOU GET THE NOTES UP HERE** & a fat black kid throws a lemon at us. Just before the lemon reaches the cloud it turns into a neon yellow bird, then into a note that lands a few feet from us on cloud.

019: I'm really scared. I never wanted to be a cop. Do you think people hate us. Because we are cops in love. Yes. Probably.

020: I wanted a better life for us. I didn't want us to

end up in these clouds with 198 other cops. That's what I'm thinking as the cops take turns jumping from the cloud & into the lemon trees where the black kids are waiting with pitchers of lemonade.

021: I wanted to be less angry at your angry cop eyes.

022: The lemon trees have grown tall but not tall enough. Most of the cops land in the trees & they get cut, maybe break ribs. A few cops miss & land on the grassy field. A group of black kids wearing neon blue shorts run over & drag the dead cop bodies away.

023: I wanted to be a marathon runner. I wanted to be a masseuse for dogs. A hot dog eating champion. Stuffed animal designer. I wanted to love you. You did. Yes, I did. Jump?

024: The air can do terrible things. It can cut open your cop uniform. It can make you believe in the safety of lemon trees. As we fall, I say to you: **LOOK AT THE WAVING BLACK KIDS IN NEON PINK SHORTS**. You say to me: **AFTER WE LAND I WANT TO MAKE LEMON MERINGUE PIE.**

025: I eat the grass from your mouth. Your cop eyes look so loving.

END

DEVIN GRIBBONS
A SHORT STORY

I wrote a story in which I solved all the problems in the Middle East. But only for a few seconds. Then there was trouble again.

* * *

The story was a failure. It just didn't work. Each sentence was a physical struggle and the dialogue didn't so much flow as amble along. The characters were uncooperative and even the punctuation just didn't seem right. I would have discarded the work completely but I liked the idea too much. As for the words, I could not have cared less about them.

* * *

The story was called A Short Term Solution. It was written in the present tense.

The past tense is typically the tense chosen to tell a story, as it lends weight to the words. It gives them a sense of historicity. The future tense is almost never used for story telling. It is a tense of possibilities, maybe even a tense of hope, but certainly not of stories.

I chose the present tense because it is the tense of the moment. And that's what I was attempting to capture in the story. A moment.

* * *

Much of what I am writing now is in the past tense, with the present tense sprinkled in here and there for a bit of flavor. However, the very last line will be in the future tense. So was that one.

* * *

The story had opened with me rebuking the reader. "Where?" the reader asked.

"Somewhere," I had replied.

"When?" the reader had then asked.

"Irrelevant," I had scolded.

The reader then thought for a moment before asking "How? And Why?"

"These are better questions, but still they don't matter," I had said.

* * *

The reader, of course, could not actually ask me those questions. I had only pretended they had. Really, I was just talking to myself.

* * *

I eventually did get around to telling the reader what mattered. What I said was this:

"Three will be sacrificed in a country of sacrificers. One is tainted. One is disillusioned. But one, one is pure."

* * *

The country that I referred to was Israel, though this was never revealed in the story. The three sacrifices that I mentioned were the majority of the characters in the story, though it was the one that was pure, and the man who picked her to be sacrificed, that took up the majority of the work. It was supposed to be a love story of sorts.

* * *

At one point in the story, I instructed the reader to look upon that man. I went so far as to tell them to touch him. To smell him. I prodded the bravest of the readers to open the man's head and peer inside. I told them to take a visit into his unconscious, to watch the man's most lurid sexual fantasies like they were nothing more than late night cable.

* * *

The man's name was Gabriel and he was a soldier in the Israeli army. He had been given the duty of selecting someone to be executed in response to an attack that had taken place earlier that day. The attack was not described in detail. I simply explained it as this:

"The enemy is a time bomb waiting to go off. And he does. The explosion rips through the sounds of the day: the grinding of automobiles, the shouts of peddlers showing their wares, the chatter of people as they stroll the marketplace. There is only the roar. And fire. Those that survive, scream and huddle for cover. Those who do not, remain silent. What is there left to say? Miraculously only three die, but many are wounded. Surely three more will die."

I got to them soon enough.

* * *

The attacker was never given a name. In fact he was never mentioned again. He had strapped himself with explosives and blown himself to pieces. It was to be up to the reader to pick them up and put them together, should they wish to know his tale. A messy job.

* * *

The attacker had been a religious extremist, but more importantly he had been a Palestinian. The word Palestinian was never mentioned in the story. Nor was the word Jew. The Palestinians were simply referred to as the Enemy. The Jews were referred to as either Soldiers or Civilians, depending on their profession. I didn't want the reader to get bogged down in the politics, the way I was getting bogged down in the words.

* * *

In the story, the Israeli government had created a law that required one Palestinian to be executed for every Jew killed in a Palestinian attack. Israeli soldiers would simply walk through the streets and pick whomever they wanted. Men. Women. Children. It didn't matter. None were above the law. "An eye for an eye. A tooth for a tooth. A life for a life. So it has been written and so shall it be," the makers of the law had said.

* * *

There was a problem with the law, however. It was not just the obvious ethical dilemma of blaming an entire people for the attacks of some. Such moral qualms could easily be silenced with a time-tested recipe of prejudice and fear. Rather, in the story, the law did not work. The attacks on the Jewish people did not stop or even reduce in frequency. Nor did Palestinians seem perturbed when they were chosen for execution.

This is why. In the story, the Palestinians were not afraid of death. They believed that everyone that was executed was a martyr and would be rewarded beyond their wildest dreams in the afterlife. They truly believed that what they would receive in death was far greater than anything they would receive in life. A shame.

* * *

In the story, however, the policy was kept in place. I was careful to explain why this was so. I did so in a single word. That word was Justice.

* * *

It was not the intention of the story to place blame on either party. Both were just looking for a home, something that all human beings should be entitled to. Life, liberty, and a place to call home. Amen.

* * *

In the story, Gabriel fell in love with the one of the sacrifices. The sacrifice's name was Rafa. Gabriel fell in love with her the very moment he laid eyes upon her, even though she was not beautiful. It was not apparent what kept her from being so, however. Gabriel had thought her eyes might be too big, or too brown, or her smile too assured, but had never been able to figure out what exactly it was. Neither could I and I had created her.

* * *

The other sacrifices were not beautiful either, though it was clear what kept them from being so. The first was a man named Qays. He was a towering six foot six, though the hard muscles that had once covered his body were hidden under a thick layer of flab. He was exceedingly ugly, not just on the outside, but on the inside as well. When he was approached by Israeli soldiers, he assumed they were coming to arrest him because he had attempted to rape a young girl in a back alley that day. He had only stopped when an Israeli soldier had spotted him. He had not even heard about the attack.

* * *

The soldier who had seen him was Gabriel. Qays had fled as soon as Gabriel had appeared. In the story Gabriel had not chased after him, instead checking to see that the girl was unharmed. The girl had been Rafa. Oh what a tangled web I wove.

* * *

When the soldiers arrested Qays, they had no idea about the attempted rape. They had simply selected him as an excellent candidate for death. When he resisted, things went quite badly for him. Good.

* * *

He was savagely beaten by the soldiers. "He feels like he is caught in a pinball machine," I had written. "He is slammed on all sides. Every time his head is struck there is a flash of light. He swears he can hear the wail of sirens, the clanging of bells, the thud of bumpers. He imagines the point total climbing higher and higher, until infinity. Until death."

When he was executed, his face was so swollen that it looked like it was made by a child out of modeling clay. It was a face not even a mother could be proud of.

* * *

The other man's name was Tamam, and no mother would have been quick to take credit for his face either. He had helped to plan the attack that had taken place earlier that day. While preparing the explosives, one had gone off in his face. One of his eyes had been destroyed, and the skin was missing in several places. Most of his injuries were covered in heavy white bandages. He made no attempt to resist when he was arrested and acted as if he was unafraid. This would change. Before he died, he pissed himself in terror.

* * *

The soldiers that arrested him did not know of his involvement in the bombing. In the story, the soldier who had picked Taman had called him an "ugly son of a bitch." That was why they had chosen him. Because his face was repulsive and deformed from his injuries.

The soldiers knew it was easier to destroy something ugly.

* * *

The bombing that Tamam had planned had been the first attack in nearly a month. This was because, in the story, the Israelis had made a discovery that had made the Palestinians afraid of death by execution more than anything else. They had discovered how to destroy a person's soul. Stand in awe of the miracles of science.

* * *

In the story, I did not overwhelm the reader with the complex scientific details nor the intricate workings of metaphysics that were involved in destroying a human soul. It was obscenely complicated, and I must admit that I myself had only a tentative understanding of it all.

The act involved a very rare type of crystal that could only be found in Israel. When light was refracted through it, it formed an intense beam that was capable of destroying souls but had little other practical use.

* * *

In the story, this property was discovered quite by accident by an Israeli scientist examining crystalline structure. It had come at the price of the souls of two of his young lab assistants, and though their deaths were mourned, progress marched on.

* * *

The Israeli government had instantly seen the value of such a process. The Palestinians believed it was a person's soul, not their physical body, which went to the afterlife. If the soul was destroyed, they could not possibly go to the afterlife. Instead, their being would simply cease to exist. For the Palestinians, it was a harrowing prospect. It scared the violence right out of them.

* * *

The Israelis made no secret of their discovery, publicly announcing that they would be using it at the executions. They hoped never to have to make good on their threat, rather that the fear of it would simply end the violence between the two groups. And in the story, it worked. Sort of. The attacks immediately stopped and a peace fell over the land. But it was a tenuous peace, one based upon fear. Such a peace cannot hold, and when it breaks, it comes crashing down with all the weight of the world.

* * *

Gabriel was aware of all this when he picked Rafa to be sacrificed. I use the word "pick" now, but in the story he didn't so much as pick her as she picked herself. "Why?" Gabriel had asked her.

"Because," she had said. "If you don't pick me, you will pick someone else."

"But don't you deserve to live more than others? More than murders and rapists? More than those who make violence a way of life?'

Rafa's answer to this was rather remarkable. It was intended to be one of the most important lines of the story. What she said was this.

"Everyone is equally entitled to life. No one more. No one less."

✳ ✳ ✳

I find that sentence to be particularly embarrassing. It reduces a complex issue to something dumbly simplistic, and in the story, I presented it to the reader as truth. That was yet another problem. I gave Rafa all the answers, but in real life, I had none.

✳ ✳ ✳

Gabriel of course argued vehemently with Rafa, but in the end, he gave in to her wishes. There is no winning an argument with a woman. This is especially true when she is your soul mate, as was the case with Gabriel and Rafa.

✳ ✳ ✳

At some point in the story, I revealed to the reader that not every person had a soul mate but that many were lucky to have one. However, there were very few who were lucky enough to actually find theirs. They were sometimes separated by vast distances and might not even speak the same language. It was unfortunate for Gabriel and Rafa that they found each other the same day that Rafa was to die. But then again, they were still luckier than most.

✳ ✳ ✳

I also revealed that souls were not mated because they were identical. Far from it. Nor were they like jigsaw pieces that need one another to be complete. Instead, they were mated because they complement each other perfectly. It was like cosmic peanut butter and cosmic jelly coming together.

*** *** ***

Later in the story, when Rafa's soul was destroyed, Gabriel felt a strange sensation, like something inside him was trying to fight its way out. That tugging feeling was Gabriel's soul trying to follow its mate into nonexistence. Having found its complement just hours before, it could not stand the thought of being without it. It was unsuccessful though. A soul cannot commit suicide. That is a special privilege granted only to the body.

*** *** ***

During their argument, Gabriel asked Rafa why she was not afraid to have her soul destroyed. "There is nothing to be afraid of," Rafa had replied.

"Exactly," Gabriel had responded. "There is Nothing to be afraid of."

*** *** ***

Nothing was exactly what a lot of the Palestinians were afraid of in the story. They were more afraid of it than anything else. "You cannot put a price on a man's soul," Tamam's father had said when his son had expressed his outrage that the Palestinian freedom movement had come to a grinding halt at the Israeli's new threat. A simple and cliché thing to say, for sure, but there are times when clichés are the best vehicles for truth. I believe this might have been one of them.

"Not even for freedom?" Taman had asked his father in the story.

"Not even freedom," his father had replied.

* * *

Gabriel himself was free to make decisions but often did not do so. At one point in the story he told Rafa the meaning behind his name. He explained that he was named after the Angel Gabriel, who in the Old Testament was the Angel of Judgment. He was also the angel that was supposed to carry out the Will of God.

Rafa had then asked him if that's what he thought he was doing.

"I don't know," was all he had replied.

* * *

There was something else Gabriel didn't know. While the Biblical Gabriel had been the Angel of Judgment in the Old Testament, he had been the Angel of Mercy in another book. Gabriel did not know this because he had never read it. That book was the New Testament. It was the sequel to the Old Testament.

This was why the idea of taking Rafa and running away had never crossed his mind. It never occurred to him that he had another option than what he had been told to do. He could only see one side of the coin. It wouldn't have matter anyways, though. Rafa never would have agreed to leave. She would have said that if they fled, then someone else would be sacrificed.

How do I know this? Because that's how I would have written it.

* * *

There was something I didn't know when I wrote the story. I found out about it only after I had completed it. After I had cast it off as a failure.

The Biblical Gabriel had a third role. Islam taught that it was Gabriel who revealed the Qur'an to the prophet Muhammad. The Qur'an was their holy book. Gabriel, it would seem, had been a very busy angel.

* * *

In the Qur'an, it is revealed that on the final day of Judgment, the day when the whole world finally gets what's been coming to it, that it will be Jesus who deems who is deserving of salvation.

Though people often forget, since he is such a revered figure in Christianity, Jesus was born a Jew. He died one as well. That means that Muslims believe that it is a Jew that will come to judge them in the end. Imagine that.

* * *

In the story, the execution took place in public, right in the middle of Jerusalem. It was the same city where Jesus had been killed. The Romans that had executed him had not known how to destroy his soul, so they had nailed him to a cross instead. And just like for Jesus, thousands and thousands of people came to watch. Both Jews and Palestinians stood side-by-side watching. There was no fighting. The people just stood there in muted expectation. Nothing brings people to-gether more than a bit of violence.

* * *

In the story, Qays, the attempted rapist, was the first to be executed. He stood on a platform right next to Rafa. His eyes were swollen shut, however, so he could not recognize her as the girl he had tried to rape. The rest of his face was so battered, that Rafa did not recognize him either.

* * *

When Qays was killed, there was a concentration of light, a fine razor beam that was shown onto his chest. Then his soul was destroyed.

* * *

In the story, I described it as if a thousand chil-dren's balloons were popped in the same instance. I did not mean that the sound was the same, for there was no sound. Rather, I was speaking of the sudden-ness and the violence of it.

Qays' soul was represented by a thick, black light that poured from his nose, mouth, and ears. It rolled over the crowd like a wave of ink and just kept going until it was out of sight. When it had left him, his body collapsed. He was dead.

* * *

Those who were touched by Qays' soul were over-come for a moment with feelings of selfishness and wickedness, the sudden belief that the only life that should be valued was their own. Gabriel was one of those who was touched by it. The feeling lasted only an instant but afterwards, he wanted nothing more than to take a shower.

* * *

Tamam was the next to be killed. His soul was a grayish color and those it touched were overcome with anger and the desire to avenge, a righteousness that could only result in violence. This too only lasted a moment.

* * *

Rafa was the last to be killed. Her soul was a pure white color. As it touched the people in the crowd, they were filled with a sense of selflessness. It was as if the problems of the world no longer seemed too daunting to face, that the differences that had kept the Jews and Palestinians separate were petty and could at that moment be overcome. Again, the feeling lasted only a moment.

* * *

In the story, the crowd went their separate ways. It was to end with Gabriel turning to go home. The last line was this:

"Gabriel leaves, not feeling much of anything at all."

* * *

As I said, the story was a failure. Just like Gabriel could not tell why Rafa was not beautiful, I am still not sure why it didn't work.

Maybe it was because some of the dialogue seemed

forced. Or that Rafa just seemed too perfect to be real. Or maybe it was that I used the present tense in an effort to capture a moment, but the moment had somehow eluded me.

* * *

It could be that I just took on too much. I tried to take control of a situation that was out of my control. In a sense I was trying to play God even though I was terribly miscast for the part. But then sometimes I wonder if that is all that writing is. Just dicking around at being God.

* * *

I think the real root of my discontent, though, is buried in the ending. I didn't have a conclusion in mind when I began the story. I had only an idea and allowed the story to dictate itself. I allowed events to flow logically. Realistically. I was as much an observer as a writer. Perhaps I had hoped things would end differently. Happily.

* * *

Next time I will write it different.

CHRISTINA KLOESS
THE HARDEST BUTTON

There are thirteen children in the house the day the baby gets born alive. He is heaved up onto a sickening pile of dirty gray sheets and crusty towels, between fine white porcelain dishes downy with the fuzzy of new green mold.

"Name him Kelly," the thirteen children yowl. Their voices echo from behind the crummy basement door. Mother shut them down in the cellar before the baby got born. In the old house, the paint is peeling in all the rooms and the ceilings drip yellow rainwater, but the basement door still has that thick black padlock from when Grandpa was alive.

Mother wipes her sweaty forehead and deftly clips the seething umbilical cord, one-handed. Her fingers are swift and nimble; this is, after all, child number fourteen. Fourteen, she thinks to herself as she digs hanks of black hair out of her eyes. Her cheeks are sunk deep and her skin feels clammy and pale in a veneer of yellow waxy death and old age. Fourteen, Mother thinks to herself.

Kelly starts a wail, pulling in deep air. The wallpaper is peeling off the walls in big, thick strips; the walls bend and groan; wind tears through the house in a hot and furious cavalcade; Kelly wails and howls and moans.

Kelly Graham Baby McCommune. The third, Mother adds after a second of sweaty thought. Her sheets are tangled around her legs in a twining serpentine spiral. Scarlet blood is blossoming slowly across the starched outer limits of the bed dressing, starting between her legs and licking out toward the borders of the hearty walnut frame. Grandpa carved the birthing bed when he was seventeen, for Ma McCommune to heave her family into the world. Now Mother is heaving out her own family, puking mewling brats with pink faces and clenched, bratty fists; foreheads wrinkled in the concentration of deep despair and greed.

"Shut it, Kelly Graham," Mother tells the baby, and tosses the umbilical cord over her right shoulder for luck. It spatters against the wall, a deep and disturbing hollow sound that Mother does not pay any attention to.

The minute the discordant cord hits home, Tiger crawls in the bedroom window, pushing past the gauze curtains special-ordered from the Sears catalogue. His bare chest scrapes against the rough wood of the windowsill. His beaded cotton jacket catches on a silver sliver before it tears with a long and musical rrrrrrriiiiip. He sniffs the wall carefully, then hunches, picks at the umbilical cord with flattened fingers.

"Oh Tiger," Mother moans after she notices Tiger. It takes her a moment to see him, because Tiger is powerful deceptive. His mottled skin hides him seamless against the splinters and cracks of the floorboards. When she hears Tiger snuffling around the umbilical cord, Mother lets her head slump against the starched pillows. "Oh Tiiiiger. Fourteen, Tiger. Fourteen."

"Fourteen ain't so bad," Tiger deliberates. He breaks off the tip of the umbilical cord with his flattened fingers and raises the red-black-brown lump to his lips. They are cracked from the hot sun outside. He is glad to get indoors in the cool of Mother's bedroom, taking refuge from the piercing heat. "Fourteen ain't so bad. My ma had fifty-six claw outta her before she got spent on her back. Number fifty-six being what did her in."

"Who was number fifty-six? I forget." Mother raises her arm and lets it flow back down onto the blood flower sheet, limp, loose. A wet rubber band slapping lazy against hot concrete.

Tiger grins, all teeth, all yellow. Three rows. "Me." He shoves the lump of umbilical cord through his skinny lips and chews ponderously. Inside his mouth, his tongue curls rapturously over the morsel, relishing the coppery taste.

Mother raises herself gingerly on one elbow, hand pressed against her forehead. Her face is like a colicky lily, white and blotchy and hot. "Tiger. Come check the baby."

Tiger grunts and pushes himself away from the floor, limbs hanging loosey-goosey beside his ribs. His flattened fingers twitch as he walks. Standing sentinel over the bed, he nervously licks his right eyeball, hating babies and hating the wet milky stench that flows off them in nauseating waves. Mother lies slumped against the pillows, half erect and half submerged in the puddle of white and red. Tiger's flattened fingers, twitching while he stands still, hover over the baby for a heartbeat. Then he flips it over, quick, breathless.

Tiger studies carefully the stumpy features of Kelly Graham Baby McCommune. Baby stretches out on his back, wormy limbs waving furiously in octopus undulations, and Tiger stands still and straight and twitching. The lazy swipe of baby's screaming mouth, an angry gaseous gash in his face. The black pits of baby's beady eyes. His beady eyes--and then. Sudden. Eyeballs roll back into his head, leaving blacks where there should be whites. And on baby's forehead, his wrinkled baby forehead, stamped out like a return to sender label: a spiral.

"Oh Mother," Tiger moans breathless. His twitching fingers fail him, draw away from Kelly baby like a hot lizard. He doesn't want to make Mother cry, but there it is, plain as paint. The thick black spiral, like a snake, like a twisty sooty bed sheet, like a fat sleek pillbug. "Oh Mother."

Mother squeezes her eyes shut, half erect and half submerged. She can feel the thrumming heat of her heartbeat in her chest. The thirteen children are yowling behind the basement door. Tiger is breathless, his twitching fingers beating a nervy tattoo against the hollow tubes of his ribs. And Mother is spent and sweaty and now she is frightened. The heavy lusty howl tearing out of little baby lungs is dark and deadly and full of sinister deep entendre. Tearing through the peeling wallpaper and molded plaster of the house. Tearing into Mother's head. She knows what Tiger is seeing, she can see the heavy and thick heft of the spiral hovering in front of her eyes, a horrible vision.

"Kill it, Tiger," she whispers.

"Oh Mother," Tiger moans breathless, his twitching fingers following repetitious in rapid Morse code. "Oh Mother, Mother; oh Muh thur, Muuuthuuur, Mother Mother Mother."

"Kill it, Tiger," she whispers.

"Oh, Mother," Tiger moans breathless, and he grabs the baby quick, picking it up, lightning quick mitts. He grabs the baby quick and swings back, swings back, pulls back. Tiger dashes the baby against the mirror.

Again.

Mother lies shaking in the bed. The children scream.

"Kill it, Tiger."

Again.

And once the baby is dead, it is unnamed and unmade, and Mother pulls herself out of bed. The space between her legs aches in a black hollow hurt that knows no name. Her nimble fingers tease out the bloody sheets, balling up the evidence, stuffing it away, face numb and waxen and curious dead.

Tiger's breath sobs out of his throat, his nervous twitching fingers painted pulpy and red. He shudders back tears, wipes his faces with his wrist, but he can feel sobs building behind his teeth, his three rows of teeth. Shards of a mirror dig into his hand, fierce little needles. He sobs and slumps against the wall, the mirror fixed in his mind: the smooth untraceable surface, the wet shatter and the flattened scream. And the spiral hovering over it all, a black cloud of smoke. Tiger curls his long loosey-goosey arms around his shoulders, his flattened fingers fastening onto the beaded cotton of his jacket. His bare chest is slick with blood and he is wishing that he could get the coppery taste out of his ugly vile mouth.

"Children," Mother yells at the basement door, her hands steady and curious dead. "Children, shut your faces. There was no baby. There is no baby."

Tiger groans, twisted and wretched.

Mother turns quick to him. Her face is white like bone. A flat arid breeze whispers through the holes in the house, stirs her lank black hair around her chin like dead lazy lilies around a pond.

"Get up, Tiger," she says to Tiger, huddled against

the wall, his face wet with tears. "There is no baby. Go and wash your hands. There was no baby. Go and wash up."

JAMES YEH
YOU DON'T NEED A PLACE TO
SLEEP IF YOU DON'T PLAN ON
SLEEPING, OR 5 SHORTS

OWL SERVICE

The bumpy ride back I liked to stare at the empty brown seats and listen to the whir of the electric motor. Hills, the angled and winding street, headlights, rain. One night a couple got on, drunk and carrying a bunch of stuffed animals. Looking at them I imagined myself in a moment like that, being so happy. I asked how they'd gotten so many toys. Turns out the guy had won them in one of those machines with the claw in it.

You must be pretty good, I told him.

There's a trick to it, he said. He paused, as if considering whether to share his secret. He started to tell me but halfway through, I lost interest and began to think about something else.

What was it I was thinking about? And what did he say? Something about moving the sliding thing around, working the way the claw is positioned. I can't remember. It was disappointing. The lack of mystery; the simple method and formula. I regretted asking.

I AM FREQUENTLY WRONG

I was so sure it was something new, or else something I hadn't felt in a while, but it was hard to tell with somethings, particularly the kinds of somethings I was so sure about. I was frequently wrong. But this was only realized in hindsight. And who's to say? Who are you and I to call both the before and during as something that was wrong, based solely on what little we do know, which is the after? When you were ready to go, I walked you home. I remember the coat you were wearing, which was shapeless, like a lump of potatoes. It was cold that night walking you back to your apartment, but I didn't mind. I could never tell you about it, but I had a dream that night and you were in it.

Your cool cheek and beautiful, soft mouth.

A throttle in the heart.

Years go by.

SCENE WITH FAMILY, AT FAMILY RESTAURANT AND BUFFET

I sat for dinner at Family Restaurant and Buffet with family and extended family, staring at a tall girl who had come in with her mother and little brother as we ate our food and yelled at each other about something I do not wish to relate, something about misunderstanding and responsibility, or something not.

My cousin had started up yelling at his mother, my father had started up yelling at my cousin, my mother had started up yelling at my cousin but for a different reason, my other cousin at her brother for their sister...

What was this? Where was I? I looked around. At the table next to us, a child had a stuck a pair of chopsticks up his nose. There they hung, thin wooden boogers. The tall girl who had walked in with her mother and younger brother was now standing at the register, saying something to the dyed-haired girl who worked there. The girl and her mother were looking through the menu and pointing at things as the girl's brother hopped around next to them, making his shoes light up.

In a quiet, yet insistent voice, my mother said something to my cousin.

Why you talk, snapped my father.

Why *you* talk, snapped my mother.

Can't you just shut up? said my father.

Can't say anything to him, said my mother, to me.

Just then a stack of clean plates arrived. We stopped yelling to switch out our dirty plates. We continued eating for a while. Then someone spilled something on the tablecloth and my father started to yell about that too. I looked at the child, whose chopsticks were now in the sides of mouth, pointing down like walrus teeth. I looked at the girl, who was now walking out after her little brother and mother, large puffy bags of food, dangling from their hands.

What would you have done? Would you have gone out after them, as I have and continue to do, out of that restaurant and into the rest of the night?

By the time I got out of there, the girl and her family were all gone, nowhere to be found. I searched as far as I could see, up and down the dark-hilled streets, but to no avail.

Picture going back to your aunt's, everyone now sitting around quietly eating pastries.

Picture playing video games with your cousins for a while, stretched out across a giant brown sofa.

A TERRIBLE GIRLFRIEND

We were at the bar, sitting on the same side of the booth.

Let me tell you something, I said and kissed your ear.

Let me tell you something else, I said and kissed your other ear. You had nice ears. I had fallen in love with your nice ears.

Let me tell you something better, I said and was prevented from kissing your ears, by you.

OTHER TIMES

It all changes like this:

Downstairs the girl's mother is frying shrimp and her father is watching the game. Upstairs the door is closed but still unlocked, a rule of theirs when she has company. Her back sliding across the carpeted floor, a trail of friction marks where we've been. Our jeans around our ankles. We are blocking the doorway, heads pressed up against the door and holding our breath. The radio is on. She asks me if I know the song that's playing and I shake my head. She asks me if I hear something downstairs and I say no. She looks at me for a second and I kiss her. I tell her she should stop worrying, that everything will end up fine.

She asks me if it feels good and I nod.

TODD SEABROOK
WHEN ROBIN HOOD FELL WITH AN ARROW THROUGH HIS HEART

Alan-a-Dale sits cross-legged in the crux of the oak tree roots. The back of his Lincoln green tunic has rotted into the bark, and insects have burrowed into his spinal tissue. Even though he is still alive, a colony of ants slowly excavate one of his lungs, their procession funneling into the hole between his ribs and carrying out pink chucks of sponge and cartilage on their backs. We watch them move over the leaves and disappear into the black ground. There are no prayers anymore, even at a burial. One of Alan's eyes is swollen shut and oozes green puss; the other never closes. Even his gangrene is a shade of Lincoln, which matches his hat, which matches our tunics. A disintegrating lute sits in his lap, moaning a single note from a single gut-string. All the other strings have snapped, and this one will break too, soon. The wood has splintered and the neck has warped so much the string slumps into a low arch. The sound is the chipping away
                            of Alan's finger bone as he grinds it against a knot in the wood, looking for invisible sounds. There is a pile of fingernails next to his boot heel—another nail just fell off, a dead leaf falling in this shrinking forest. He only has two left, and he will probably die before they go.   A person can only go on for so long. For eight days we tried to feed him, then stopped because he swallowed all his teeth and his gums wouldn't stop bleeding. We told him that no one had collected the reward yet. No one seemed to know who did it. He didn't move when a badger gnawed through

his boot and took one of his toes away. We tried to scare him by shooting arrows into his hat, but Alan-a-Dale just sat there with moss growing up his legs, a termite nest in the bend of his knee, staring at the spot whyre Robin Hood fell with an arrow through his throat.

For three days Will Scarlett shot arrows into the air waiting for one to come down on him. He stood in a small clearing, shooting the arrows straight up, often times bending so far backward his quiver would spill its contents onto the grass. The bow twangs could be heard at the castle walls, ever encroaching, and the air would hiss as the arrows passed the treetops. When they came back down, the shafts would bury themselves an elbow's length into the ground or stick into the surrounding trees. Skewered birds fell out of the branches like acorns. On the first day when the wind snagged an arrow at its apex, it came down on a hart's skull more than two hundred yards away. The meat lasted us for four meals since there weren't that many of us left. One of us died trying to give Scarlett a bowl of venison stew to maybe keep him alive. But an arrow pinned the man's brain to his tongue from twenty feet away. Perfectly good stew spilled everywhere. We had to drag the body out with shields over our heads in order to bury him. After that we let Scarlett be, not coming any closer than eye-shot. A few of us took bets to see if we could shoot off Will's quiver strap from that distance, but not one of us came within thirty yards. Most of us hadn't even strung our bows since Robin Hood fell with an arrow through his throat. The form starts to go when it hasn't been used, even for Merry Men. Scarlett didn't speak to anyone, not even to Little John as he passed by for the final time. When Scarlett ran out of arrows, he would either pull them from the ground or fashion new ones from dead ash and cardinal feathers. On the second day an arrow put a hole in the bill of his hat and another pinned his foot to the forest floor.

He pulled it out, blood squirting like a geyser, notched it to his string and fired it into the air. The third day he caught himself in the thigh as he bent to scavenge arrows. His Lincoln green pants turned black with the blood. Later that evening an arrow shaved off Will Scarlett's left ear, broke through his collar bone and pierced his heart. He remained upright for a few moments, letting the bow slip from his calloused fingers. Finally, his knees buckled and he collapsed.

The wall
already be
to disir
while they e

Much the Miller's son hangs in a noose, his bare feet pointing outward and his britches soiled. Although his hands are tied behind his back, his   fingers were already broken by the Sheriff and still stick out at odd angles like a mangled thistle bush. The broken capillaries in his wrists congeal under
his skin, the liquid swelling his joints
like sausages. His bow was auctioned
off awhile ago. The town's children
spit on his corpse, and the women
throw rocks. The beggars watch.
Some of us watch separately, undisguised
and from the safety of the woods, as that is how close the stone walls are these days. Robin Hood would have saved him with some bait-and-switch plan or a convoluted ambush, maybe run the Sheriff through and snatch the guard's own purses in the process. But Robin Hood is dead and we are the only ones left.
We discuss elaborate plans to retrieve Much's body for burial, mighty escapades, legendary even, but we are a dwindling gang, such merry men we were, and do not have the gutting nerve that we once did. We talk and talk, the words slowly draining from us, until we can't understand each other anymore. We walk through the Nottingham gates, freshly cut and towering, unhinge Much, and walk out with his body.

Little John walked away.
We saw him throw his bow and staff onto the fire, the same ones
with which he beat Robin, then turned on his heel and limped
west toward Barnesdale. Away from Nottingham. Out of Sherwood
Forest. He walked in a straight line, something that was once
impossible in Sherwood. The forest used to be dense, suffocated
with oaks and ash trees. It once took Friar Tuck a year and half to
cross from one side to the other. Of course, he got lost, but Robin
Hood could do it in a day. Now Sherwood Forest is shrinking, losing
ground to the Nottingham market and the Barnsdale tournament
fields. It cringes in the presence of
the castle walls. We see passing freely all the monks and the fryers,
the pinders, the potters,
the knyghts and the beggars,
the kyngs and the lovers,
all on hir way to Notynggam.
The trees slink away. The underbrush withers. Kirkley Nunnery
cleared trees for a new stable. All the game has been hunted out
and we are beginning to starve along with Alan-a-Dale. Someone
suggested that we collect the reward for killing Robin Hood, but
that's how Much got caught.
He walked into Nottingham and was
arrested immediately, charged with poaching, either King Richard's
deer or the Prince of Thieves, we aren't sure which. The reward
would have meant enough cured meat for a month, although that's
not why Much did it. Who did it? That was the question we kept
asking.
Who did it? Who fired a birch arrow into the air that missed

everything else in the world, and killed our lowly Robin Hood? If the assassin wanted the reward he would have to come forward when Much tried to claim it. No one came forward. Of course, that's not really why Much did it either. Will Scarlett, Little John, Alan, now Much; sometimes there is no difference between a person and his surroundings. Little John had lost fifty pounds and shrunk half a foot before the stroke hit him. Half his body went dead and his beard stopped growing on one side of his face, while the other side turned grey and grew faster. Little John didn't say anything when he passed Will Scarlett shooting arrows into the sky, even when a falling shaft took off one of Lytell Johnn's fingers at the knuckle. He walked for days. We could still see his Lincoln green all the way to Exeter.

There ThereThyre is nowhyre to hide anymore. There

The Sheriff of Nottingham is locked inside the castle. When he strung up Much the Miller's son, it wasn't for poaching, or outlawdry, it was to prove that Robin Hood, that the Prince of Thieves,

wasn't dead. Locking Much in gaol and excusing the gaoler, the Sheriff stayed up all night, watching the cell from behind a stack of wine barrels, waiting for the rescue. We even knew that and still couldn't come up

with a plan. The next morning he paraded Much

all the way

across Nottingham,

twice, stopping every

now and then

to break a finger,

expecting Much

to admit that Robin Hood was still alive. As he levered the knuckles against the handle of his sword and snapped them back, one by one, Much didn't make a sound. The sound of the bones popping echoed all the way to the high tower where a guard threw up his breakfast. After the fourth finger, the Sheriff lost interest and had someone else break the rest. On the gallows the Sheriff did a dramatic countdown before he kicked out the trapdoor. Much jerked against the rope, twisting his body like a fish. The Sheriff had his sword drawn.

When the body stopped writhing
and Robin Hood hadn't show up,
when no one threw off their cloaks or pulled a sword from a pile of firewood, the Sheriff shuffled off the gallows, bumping the swinging body, and hurried back to the castle with a look of panic on his face.

Although things had already begun to break down, he declared an archery contest to be held the next day by the north tower. Couriers were sent out to the surrounding villages, calling for the best archers to compete for a silver arrow. When we retrieved Much during the night we could hear the Sheriff sharpening his dagger on a whetstone and yelling at his staff. Every hour or so we could hear a piece of the castle wall crumble, which in the morning would leave a dip in the straight line of stone. Each corner of the wall was a perfect 90 degrees, which seemed to become sharper each day. Until it crumbled.

Whyn no one showed up for the tournament, the Sheriff stormed into the market and jammed the silver arrow into a potter's shoulder who was laying out his wares. Whyn the Sheriff asked why no one showed up they said they didn't know which way was north, and therefore didn't know how to find the north tower. The Sheriff considered this and doubled the reward for whoever killed Robin Hood. Three hundred gold pieces. No one was fool enough to believe that the Screffe of Notynggam wanted to congratulate the archer or promote him in rank. He just wanted to find out who killed Robyn Hode.

Just like the rest of us.

Friar Tuck does geometry. He calculates the length and the width of the arrow, the type of wood, the weight, the feather balance, the iron tip adjustment. The angle of the entry wound, how far Robin Hood's body slid on the ground, the nearest deer paths. The weather conditions, the wind adjustment, Robin Hood's footprints, the weight of God, King Edward's latest decree, the line of sight to the castle walls, to the courtyard, to the Barnsdale tournament fields. All day he scribbles over the pages of his Bible using a charcoal stick, drawing straight lines with the edge of his dagger, crisscrossing them with numbers piling up in the margins. Eventually the page has so many markings, it looks like ink was spilled. Then he turns the page and starts over. He told us that he could not only calculate to the inch from where the arrow was shot, but by taking into account every variable he could tell us the exact person who shot it. From the price of mutton, the new Cardinal in Lancaster, and the movement of the stars, the Friar told us it was someone who had a red beard and has been to Normandy. The position of Alan-a-Dale sitting cross-legged against an oak combined with a southeasterly wynd meant that the archer was over eight feet tall. We haven't hearde a mass synce Robin Hood died.

Robyn Hode is dead, felled with   arrow through   throat. He
                lies in a casket made of ash   wood.
    quiver
and his bow are crysscrossed over his chest, the Lincoln green
blending   in with his clothes, although the arrows have
                                of the quiver   spilled out.
He has rotted very quickly and a spider has built a nest in the
hole in his throat and scurries in and out of it with dead insects.
One eye is still open, the other is encrusted with dirt. His beard is
matted w/
            blood from when he fell face-first into the dirt,
                        breakynge his nose.
One side of his mouth is closed like it was clamped in a vice.
The other side of
his lip rolled down when
it slid over the ground, nearly pinning it to his chin. When rigor
mortis kept it there. His face has distorted
features, one side squashed together, the other elongated in shock.
Workers dug up his grave by accident when they were
                                    putting in a foundation
for the expanded city walls. Even for the dead,
                        is nowhyre to hide   Scherewod
anymore.   We cannot even take solice in that quest. It is
becoming harder
            and harder   to keep   it   to   geth   er.
                        The Sheriff has been called so we
cannot stay here. He wants to see   the corpse with
his own eyes. He put a bounty on ure heads as well. He needs
something to do, after all.
No one
has claimed the reward, because no one wants to admit they are
the one who killed good Roben Hode-a-Dale.   We
debate being arrested.   It might be better to be hung,
pegged by rotten fruit and the nasty stares of children, instead of
wytherynge away with the forest.

But we retreat into Sherwood, passing
/tell Alan-a-Dale whosits cross-legged in the crux of the oak tree roots,
most dead, but not dead yet. Thye myghte build hym into the cornerstc
⸱ the castle wall when yt reaches him. Or maybe   mix hys remaː
.to the mortor, smoothing hym out with a trowel, whyle we keep movyr

walls are   deeper

.dy beginning   dyiing Scherewod

sintegrate even

e they expand.
                         Whyre ellse are we
          ButSc here woodIs

                              suposed   to go?   ys the
     supposed to go? The question we

     don't
          ask.   angleoftheentrywoundhowfarRobinHood'sbodyslidor
                                      groundthenearestdeerpathsweath

              Where else are we supposed to go? The question we

          not dead   yet

DANIELLE ADAIR
FROM SELMA.

3/19

I have a brother who I once told to eat carrots.
I said this to him while he was crying outside the
screen door. He was sleep-deprived and manic and
trying to quit smoking. Economists are always quitting
something, but my brother is without much and has
reason. He did. The psychotherapists in our depart-
ment tell me, "the young one," which is always quali-
fied with "serious," that what we experience in our first
seven to twenty-one years of life influences everything
thereafter. "All research is me-search," the older grads
say. Isn't all life based on the prior step? That's why
people are insomniacs. I've also heard in more wistful,
youthful rants that one is not sure of their own sexual
orientation until twenty-six. Marker. Just markers, I say.
I know why my brother doesn't sleep, and he is ten
years older. I know why I care, and it's not because I
am still "experiencing." Some people carry the weight

of others they interact with to a destructive degree. Worry becomes a burden beyond reflection in the interface between them and others. But there is a thing as too much empathy. Empathy can be pathological beyond just indulgence. It can also hurt others. That, I am finding.

3/23

You have a perception of grad school being the nexus for everyone you'll ever love or really know. You feel like you've never been adequately matched but that in higher education you will find your own kind. I took my year off. I taught abroad. I stayed pursuant on my topic. I clarified my question. I did everything they tell you in undergrad. *They* being the people who know you want to continue your schooling. *They* are also you, but they don't want to fess up to their own disappointment upon matriculation. My colleagues are clever and diverse. Some are young and others have children. But I feel restrained to tell them my goals, and I don't want to let myself discover these goals more completely through conversation.

3/30

Tonight, another Thursday at the Professor's surrounded by pizza and beer and cushions. I don't recall the Speaker's name or profession but that she said some contentious things about a program housing new Nepalese immigrants. There is something about Thursday nights that makes me feel disgusted. I always show up, skidding down the brick neighborhood streets with my tennis on and carrying an umbrella. It always rains on Thursdays. Some of my friends ask good questions. Some of them sit back and jot down. Most of us PhD students are aware of each other's expressions. It's our main focus in these first few years. Even the professors ask questions of the Speaker at times, rather than casually interjecting their assumed authority. I leave happy that I attended and full on food. Sometimes I hug my thesis advisor. Sometimes we don't even talk. But neither case is a measure. I walk out before a friend can offer me a ride, anxious to get home and ready to loose my adrenaline through walking. It always rains on Thursdays.

4/6

A Master's Thesis is really just like a gateway drug. If you are in the right state of mind you will become addicted. If you are feeling hesitation, your plan becomes a nightmare. I've known a lot of students who have dropped out. Josie's headaches were getting worse, and so she finally decided they were attributable to the faculty and their cold veneer towards her work. "The retention of stress," she kept saying, "the retention." I've replaced Josie as "the young one." Although we are the same age and her boyfriend is a pilot, Josie was my younger at social events. The faculty devours interest but distastes liveliness. My mentor, Sue, said, "Our country graduated less than a thousand PhD's last year... She'll be back," in reference to Josie. I heard the lame struggle in her words. The university has become a penitentiary containing the soured intellectuals of our future and bastardizing the Darwinian model. I think my mentor resents Kay simply because Kay lived out west. But, then, State schools always have the gall to not be bothered by the condescension of Neogothic privates.

4/8

The more I read the more I feel indicted by my convictions. The more I read, in the hollow chambers, beneath the stained glass windows and patriarchs of the old University, tangled by my legs in wooden chairs, absent of the omniscience of clocks, among the haggard deportment of colleagues or bystanders or committed lives, alongside withering book bindings and embossments that have lost their shimmer, warmed by the earth tones and chilled by the vacant air, the more I feel undeserving. Libraries love the logic of physical science. "All biologists want to be chemists. All chemists want to be physicists. All physicists want to be mathematicians. All mathematicians want to be God, and God is a biologist." No one cares about how loud they turn their pages in the library when focused on their thesis work. Being seated sinks into one's body, and people stumble in their steps. But I enjoy walking out of Harper library late at night and letting myself skip through the routine I've established for missing the cracks between cobbled stones. The walkways of the old University are like diagrams of tectonic plates. Here in the Midwest though I never have to worry about improvising my routine. These cracks are stubborn, remain large and in place. Much of my education is this way. But the walkways never make me think that they are mapping it. Instead, the stones evoke trickery, induce pretend, and I always remember watching Dorothy skip towards the horizon.

5/2

This day, the one before the first, I get a call. "It's time. When can you meet?" I am free and already know what I will wear. Driving in the car I feel transgressive or grown-up, I can't decide. I ride in the middle of the back, on a hump, and listen like a poet to the radio. My colleagues discuss with consideration how they want what is to happen to happen once the three of us arrive. I am patient. I feel clarity— She is lucky. It's not a clarity that will leave her, she thinks; Selma knows when she feels this kind of confidence. After all, it is her first day.

There's a school inside a brick building. An institution doesn't have to be concrete. It makes Selma wear a nametag. Selma spent five hours enrolling and never got to meet the other students, not until her real first day. Selma is not a molester. She hasn't done hard drugs or sold. She already knows the rhetoric of community from her studies, and she carries a degree. Selma doesn't have enough skin to get a fingerprint—she's a sculptor. Selma is allowed to bypass this part. Selma makes jokes with her colleagues, but she feels more knowing than them. Selma smiles with choreography and greets Accounting with a script. She walks around tired because that is what happens when she is nervous. She walks around wishing to just be a part and wondering to where she's led herself in. Selma is a student. Selma is already a "Consumer" in the literal sense. Selma thinks she has already got theses and has already reached terminable ends. She's just waiting to hear a bell.

Selma's first thought was to wash her hands. They were so dry though. And look, Dickie Kelly didn't care about pulling out that chair and helping Cassandra sit down. Selma wanted to be that helpful. But when Dakota slipped her his telephone number, written on the ripped-off lid of his cigarette box—the lettering looked of a fifth grade girl's hand: the "o" was as wide as the "a" and "k" together, and the ink was blue, but he had made an "a" with a curvy indentation and then just used a stick on the right to demark the other one on the end, just like how Selma switched-up the style of her capital "A's" sometimes mid-sentence, making Selma sympathetic—still she hesitated to touch the advance. Dear God, do I have a type? Is it he without being Him? Selma likes to scare herself. There's a bit of apathy that infects itself in danger and that makes some experiences seem "Smooth." Selma likes how Dakota calls himself that.

"Which chair?" 'You mean the one that Kendra was sitting in when she thought we all looked so young?' Selma loved feigning adulthood, with her colleagues, but because of her looks rather than the age that separated her from being interested in the Council as a long-term project like them. Selma never thought in "long-term" and that is, perhaps, where she went wrong. Because you can only feign honest communication with someone long enough to not realize that that is all that you are about. A fake, a hack, a prodigy, a tag-along, "serious," enough. Selma realized real young that she could see other people. Everyone pushed her into acting, indirectly. Sadly, she hadn't decoded until then, that she is good at seeing people because she is transparent. She sees through them as a need, she aches as they do as a blessing. Selma felt so misled by her upbringing, so discouraged from her fans, that she voiced heart-to-heart with Leonard one day that she is always just concocting, verbalizing a narrative like him.

"I sing because I'm happy, and I sing because I am free." That was the last time Jones spoke with Selma. He came over and asked if Selma had, "Heard this one before?" When she said she wouldn't be able to say without a sampling, Jones jumped into song. He stood only two feet opposite her chair, tilted his chin up and bowed his eyelids. Jones has tight braids striping his skull and they connect in a tail at the nape of his neck. Selma saw Jones embodying a cathedral—his whole gesture was proffering itself to someone beyond the arrangement. Selma had no illusions though. She knew where she sat and that she performed, herself, all the same. "That's a known piece." Dakota moves his focus from taking in Jones to talking to Selma. His words feel fatherly and perfectly measured. The words warm Selma and her experience of sitting under the canopy those last few moments. She understands why Dakota is a "God's Disciple," and she is happy that this he has achieved. Her first real day at the Council goes like this: Dakota motioning to Selma, "Hi Honey. Come sit down over here by me." There's interlude before he asks her about music. When he does he barely lets her respond. He says he is "Smooth." He tells her he likes rap. Jerome, nearby, peering around Dakota's grizzle, says he can rap too. Now Jerome begins to sing. He gets into it and well, but can only keep the lyrics rolling for a few rhymes to resolve. Dakota breaks in when Jerome starts to stumble and you realize, helping each other out, is a Consumer's only recourse. Dakota resurrects his peer's tune with a new scat. "And ya mama said, 'si si, si si,' your mamma said to me." The lyrics come in perfect succession. Dakota's rap seems effortless but scripted and manipulated but pungent. Selma hates herself later for not being able to recall the words as they were sung. Selma thinks she's in a movie. She knows quite well that everyone senses the height of the scene. It makes Selma remember sixth grade and dreaming at night, wishing so much that the school could burst into melody, that she'd be in a choreographed musical as the director who performs and sings. Later, later than leaving Dakota for good, an acquaintance to whom Selma disclosed this for the first time tells her that "everyone wishes the same thing." It makes Selma feel like another rip-off, another ripped-off lid, like the three men's singing that made her feel so good. They hovered around her. When Jerome faltered, Dakota took over for his own nourishment. They are dogs climbing over and around each other, unabashedly, brazenly, as if chasing a carrot. And Dakota says as he wraps up his beat, "this is how it goes."

Selma was walking around. She wanted to have someone to go up to but didn't want that someone to feel like they were her choice. She wanted to be dirty in a romantic way, like the way of books or in minds, but then she saw Samuel with his wet under-nose just starring himself off into "distant," and she was resistant to go sit down. Chairs are institutional; they are institutions. And it's funny how Selma can collocate in her thoughts but can't enunciate a slash mark though she thinks them all the time. Freud didn't have an Emes chair; his was custom-made. And Selma was happy that day when Dakota felt all the chairs before he showed her where to sit down. Selma questioned why each day ever since a chair, one chair has remained perpetually wet. To that chair, urination isn't catastrophic it is ritualized. But Selma didn't want to smell where not to sit. She didn't want her senses to invade her though they protected her own spot. The canopy for all the chairs—ones with only four spokes, the office kind that have wool fabric and come with five extensions on their wheelie base, and lawn chairs, the white plastic rounded kind, and card table chairs – made Selma realize long afterward that they were all she had to memorize to understand the institution. That one French he, that artist of hers, had written her an email about rolling around on office chairs along Pont Neuf. Damn him, damn him who makes her want to forget that she smells. He had played Selma a song with lyrics that included "a girl with smelly feet." Selma had been keeping her shoes outside the shutter doors. With her thin souls, she had walked Europe all over.

"Player Hater," that's what Dakota calls Jerome. "But why so?" Selma inquires. "You don't know. He steals my game. I got honeys, ladies, and now white chicks. He, man, he hates playas because he don't got none." "So, but, we've talked before? I thought you two were friends?" Selma colludes. "Nah, not him. Not that motha playa hater." Jerome approaches Selma and her interlocker at the canteen table. He just laughs, giggles and laughs, at and around Dakota. Dakota, putting on "man" in his response, so despondent and self-congratulating, continues looking straight. He continues to look at Selma as if still speaking, but his peripheral eyes are staring at Jerome with disgust. "Hey, man—he ain't nothing," Dakota directs to Selma. "He thinks he got a chance. Look at him as if he thinks he's something. Man," to Jerome, "you ain't nothing but a playa hata." And Selma started to cry one day at the Council. She walked around shielding her eyes by being downcast. She knew tears were not uncommon, even from Dakota, inside here. But they were for her, to them. How close can someone be, if they are tears away? Selma felt broken.

God comes about and leaves and walks around and scatters disbelief and scatters passion and he's a lot like Leonard. But Dakota told Selma that God made women with their legs spread apart because that's how "a woman like to be taken." Dakota is part of God's Disciples, but Dakota says he won't let his younger cousin be. Dakota says he doesn't deal but that he'll someday have enough money to produce his demo tape. He says that day he'll arrive and young ladies will spread out their legs and the 40,000 people in the bible will all come back. That day God will tell him he's a prophet—that's why Smooth sings. "There are demons all around us." Dakota leans into Selma and whispers this without adjusting his volume. He is 250 pounds, maybe plus, and he is six feet four, so he says, and Dickie calls him, "Chubacca." "Playa hata," Dakota mumbles in revolt. He tells Selma that Dickie was in jail for rape. He is "evil", the "incarnation", and he "needs to be in here" not just inside. If Selma can work at the Council, take notes and talk meds and even hug a Consumer, why does Dickie and Nurse Kendra and that woman in ceramics and the staff up in Accounting, choose to be here each and every day? Dickie is serving his sentence right now. He gives self-help lectures to the Consumers and talks about treatment as if it were a triangle: "You are all just slicing off the bottom edge." Selma listens instead to what

Dakota says when he speaks about religion and the Council. Dakota's qualification is uncanny. "This space is a school," he says. Marco made Selma realize this for the first. He stares at a sheet of The Commandments taped to the Common Area wall. He tells Selma he "don't know too much, just interested in learning."

This is what he says: "I tell my mamma, 'No, ma it's me. It's me ma,' but she doesn't hear. I know she doesn't hear. 'You don't.... ma, why are you throwing that milk jug at me?' She throws a milk jug right at... it hits me, my face, she throws the milk, and it splatters. And then my brother, I have a little brother and he is walking. We were only smoking leaves, you know. We were only little and we were playing pretend. You roll up tea, in tea bags, you can smoke tea bags, in leaves... We wanted to be like old guys, men. My mom's in a wheelchair. And I bang on the door, and she isn't there. No one is home, and I am locked out, and I have to get my brother. And my mom keeps yelling at me, 'You're not my son. Git. Git. You don't belong,' and throwing stuff at me. When I walk in she was thinking I was someone else, that's all. She kept hitting me and I told her, 'but mom, it's just me.' And there the milk jug hit me in the head, do you see? See, it, my head, and she kept banging, and I couldn't ...—Now, is this anyway for a kid to grow up?—... waiting, I was waiting, for my brother you see, waiting and I had to get in so

I could get my mother and we could go and we could leave." His monologue begins when Leonard peers over his shoulder in standing up. It's like he is exiting but needs a last word. This is Leonard's first explanation for his head. This is when his head got hurt first. At the party Leonard faces Selma in speaking. His words are slow and lucid – "Now is that anyway for a kid to grow up?" – as if they're the only part he truly can't believe. That day Selma feels she's finally met Leonard. And that same day, at the same party, the party for Nurse Kendra, who was graduating and leaving the Council, nothing is different at school except for the cake.

Tracey is spooky and smiling. She sways beside the table. There are various ceramic pots and ashtrays and saucers displayed. It looks archeological more than hands-on. And the woman—Selma can't remember her name, Selma wants to assume she is an, the, occupational therapist though Selma appreciates the woman's authority within the room regardless—says Tracey's "got MD." Selma nods and digests and pretends to understand, though she is fiercely trying to construct an acronym for Down's syndrome. "This is where we take the severely disturbed for activity time, and the Council shouldn't really even be helping Tracey, because we don't take people with MD." "Oh." "Her father pushes though, and there are family problems, and we realize there's no where else she's safe." Selma is still nodding. In comes Leonard with his right shoe in his hand. "I can't find the lace. I can't find it, and I think I am going to throw away my socks." The woman, Selma can't remember her name, says that Leonard has done this before. The staff once had to fish his socks out of the bins behind the Council. "Leonard, those are the only shoes you got, you better hold on to them." Selma remembers what Dakota said the other day while Leonard wandered past, "God, that's who I'm sorry for. What about him?"

"I almost hit the door," Leonard says holding his shoe. "I almost hit my head." The woman takes possession of the shoe without saying anything. This must be routine, Selma thinks as she watches the woman untie the shoe and simultaneously address Selma. "Has he told you this? He had a very bad family life growing up and his father got custody, and he has been in treatment for many years, but he's had various jobs. When—" Leonard, now winding around the only three chairs in the cramped room—there is no space for painting pottery—starts to speak more loudly, asking the room this time for its attention. Selma notices that he stands at the same angle and same distance from her as the woman does; they both look at Selma when they speak. Selma is cornered. "I have been shocked three times." "That's true," the woman interjects. "My dad put a pole to my head and that's when Jerry, remember, yeah cousin Jerry, well, you know him, re-member? And my dad they were playing ball, I don't very much like it, but I was hitting it, and I jumped too high, and the bar, it was this bar that knocked my head. It hit my head, and I was hit hard, and my head got broken right here, can't you? And Jerry made me top janitor. I liked that job, but I also was a guard and that was okay. I liked cleaning houses though— it was okay to be a janitor. That was before I got shock the second time." Selma feels like she is making sense of Leonard's story. Selma feels like she knows beyond what the woman tells her or what the woman has given up belief that she someday could. Selma feels guilty when as she thinks about how she regards herself good at understanding babies. She knows her expressions aren't outwitting her logic and making her feel that she knows what Leonard says instead of ac-tually hearing him. Unlike that one minister, the only one Selma ever heard, advised, "Smiling at everyone you meet for a month makes you a happier person," unlike that— Selma knows she's not being seduced by Leonard's story. She gets it. She gets that he's been hurt many times and that shock therapy is still the most effective, still a legal, still a repetitive treatment for mania and depression.

"I like writing. I like the way it makes me feel good. And I think it can help me. I mean, I think that if I do some more of it, it can help me work on my applications for school." Three visits later, after they'd developed a routine, one with a unique question to pose, Cassandra also said, "No," she only had that one day, "not since the workshop, five months ago when somebody came in to help teach us writing." How much longer can Selma ask, "Have you written lately?" and receive a response. Both women frequently fall into exhaustion and that's something that fueled another question that died. "Tell me about school, I mean, because you know, I am a student, and I think school is really great." "I want to go to school so that I can learn typing and other things, the necessary skills. I want to someday be a secretary at a place like this. I think that that would be a satisfying vocation and that I am getting there. I am not there yet though, it takes time to feel good, you know, but I already have my papers. I just need to finish the application papers, which takes time, you know, but I think I will manage if I keep working hard and getting well." Cassandra's words stutter like their sound in print. Each phrase takes effort. "I never liked filling out applications. They make you go through the worst part first before you even get into the school." Selma felt talking with Cassandra was taking a break. She hoped Dakota wouldn't find her. Selma was careful to sit with her back to the door and careful to slouch as if reducing her area reduces the chances of her standing out. At the same time, Selma talks less. She thinks more about Cassandra's determination, and how Dickie Kelly's triangle might prick it somehow. Sometimes Cassandra is sitting there in her chair by the window, looking like a passenger that just made it aboard with too much carry-on luggage. Out-of-breath. She is seemingly always internally struggling with compiling and filling in the blanks of a form. On the other days, most of them, Cassandra's just not there.

Selma's Smooth friend is not so much the larger Mr. Eddie. Mr. Eddie tells more convincing stories. "I know. They're all around," or "They know," he says. He nods and looks through Selma's eyes and then backs inside his padded cheeks. He cuddles into headphones and shuts his lids for "No Satisfaction." No one bothers Mr. Eddie or is bothered by him, but Dakota calls him a player hater the day Eddie tells Selma she's got beautiful eyes. "You got blue, beautiful eyes." But that was Dakota's line from before, the day everyone sang. That day had ended with a cue from inside signaling that the next session was to begin. When Selma asked Dakota if he hadn't missed it, because Jones and Jerome had both broken for the door, he told her, "Nah. That's too much like high school. I'm not in high school anymore. I don't need to go to classes." But earlier in the conversation, after "Honey" and before the chant, Dakota told Selma about eyes. "What lovely eyes you have," but Selma is excited for her story. Dakota leans in to inspect her pupils, "What are you?" "What?" "What ARE you?" he laughs, "what is your heritage?" "Umm. English. Irish." "I'm part Cherokee. I'm also Ghanaian, Norwegian, German, and I got people in Haiti." Selma thinks, Congratulations. But Selma learns that at school you need to know where you're from. It's the surest way to staving off a false but taunting "identity." Dakota—they all—hate that word, and Selma agrees: "Consumers. I don't know why they call us that. Why don't they just say what we really are?" Dakota speaks with resignation, "Patient."

"Yes. You must be you, you must be you are that now. See your eyes. You have eyes like mine. You look familiar. We look alike, don't you think? Don't you think? Yes. We should be, or we maybe we are already, you think we are related? Yes, I bet, remember Bets, remember cousin Betsy, you must. She, yeah, she is married to Mr. Reno, or maybe you know my grandmother, remember when my grandmother lived in Ohio, she used to have a picture of this little girl, Betsy, and you look a lot like Betsy, you know. Has anyone ever told you that? And that picture had this tiny little girl, she had long hair and her eyes were your color. And she is dead now, I think, I think Betsy told me that, because after grandma died the picture wasn't there. It was a black and white picture, but you would've thought she was pretty that little girl. Don't you remember Reno, he would never let me look at that picture. He thought I looked at it too much, but here you are. Here you are." "Isn't that something," Selma thinks of Dorothy Parker. Leonard recognizes her, and this is before Dakota has even sung his song. This is before Selma gets serenaded and before Selma gets called by name. This is before Selma had that first great cup of black coffee, before Selma stopped adding cream. This is when Selma sits down at a chair under the canopy and not on a bench inside. This is before the Styrofoam of a container that's topless touched her lips and before she realized that she is older now. Selma can let it count for something. Selma adjusts the station. She can't find the same song that plays inside. And in that seat, sitting there, with the moon-roof shielding the sun from entering her car, Selma sees Leonard nod to himself under the canopy. Leonard is the only white Consumer at school. No wonder Selma is his cousin.

Aesthetics are aggressive and that is why her room is black and white. But this is out of habit, not Selma's luxury. She heard the traffic engineer say something like, "A car tittering on the edge," but the woman didn't know how to decipher her own words. This is how Selma feels about many things when she walks in a space and sees how other people organize. She sees posters and pictures and eclectic things, and she feels she should know more than what she feels when these are what she's led to. In the same way, Selma is scared of the shift key and a shaky computer table. The shift button empowers, because it is long and strong and unlike her feminine demeanor. And, in her phone, the saved messages, thankfully, eventually erase, so that she will never let the power of space become key in her life. Yet, colors and fabrics and fonts in these things that she hears and sees scare Selma. And Selma has never been that interested in finding things to hang or show, except for when in preschool she'd live for the day when she could tell a story in front of her class. She would bring in the physical object to necessitate it. Selma was shy. Selma is shy. But in preschool she loved to tell stories.

Selma wanted to walk outside the confines today. She wanted to be seen in the margins. Dakota and Wyatt and a few others did. It isn't wrong to want to be an outsider in a way that's noted, not when you feel you have a right to it. But today it is raining. There is rain pouring down like a phantom itch. And it touches Selma's orb and becomes an echo of a massage upon her skin. "Do you ever get the feeling you want to cry but can't?" Cassandra turns to Selma from her seat up near the window. "Not because you're numb but because you're full of hope," she says. Her words are filled with apathy. Selma nods. Selma is too enthralled in her head to scratch at her vocal chords, but she hears Cassandra through her own loneliness. There is patience and hollowness in sitting still, and throbbing and courage in feeling warm. Sometimes these postures behold Selma and she feels still and warm in one place. Breaths later Selma lets her professionalism return and with it the viscosity that allows it to drip. Selma looks at Cassandra directly. She says, "Yes. It's like being awake but cloudy after a long sunny afternoon's nap." Rainwater is tight until it tips over itself. And you can be on the verge of tears for an entire season. Selma was until it rained.

The boy had said, "Maybe what they all need is to get a haircut." And Selma, stupid Selma, said, "I think some of them just got theirs cut, actually." How could she? "Them," Selma says about her friends. She said it out loud and in their presence. She said it and they could hear it, and she closed her ears so that she wouldn't. But Selma heard, Selma hears, and she knows what she's said. She knows it from that little man, that twelve-year-old man or the boy of and then some. He slings on the side, his bike beaten and beside him, and he has the guts to ask. He asks, "What's your nametag for?" "It means that I'm a student." She says this while tucking it beneath her unzipped jersey coat. Selma hated that badge from the beginning, wore it for all her work in filling out forms but knows it's not required. Her colleagues have lost their tags. Her co-workers don't wear scrubs or faces or look for acceptance in their clothing. Selma hates herself because she can't forget the badge. She is a good student, a good kid. She wears what she's given and what she's been told to. Selma can let herself be friends in façade and can be closer than any of her colleagues, but her nametag is a life raft. It doesn't represent privilege to Selma though—this she swears. Fuck that kid, fuck him for making her not forget that she calls them "them."

Leonard's talking relatives again, and Selma wants to keep her eyes upon him, in her selfish sense of courtesy. The kid has a brown paper bag in hand. Selma, don't think it, Selma thinks it and stops herself, and harasses herself, and undoes her own implications, and realizes there is something there to have urged her thought. The boy sips a glass bottle, a bottle because of his grip, and liquid because of the slurp of gratification in his possession of it. He is the devil, he is lurking, he's making it crazy, and she must be drunk. He is crossing the fence by looking in. He couldn't have been at the hairdresser's like he said. Selma knows this. She looks at the alley from which his bike has come, and from his slouch, and his confident curiosity reminds Selma of when Selma was biking once in the forest along a road, and a group of boys, teenagers, in a taupe colored vehicle, slowed when they rode past and yelled at Selma when parallel. They didn't care that she was young, that she was longhaired and a girl. They didn't hoot like older, lonelier men did when they saw her run by as a kid—they weren't pedophilic and Selma hated that. Selma, startled in her coast, turned her wheel the wrong way and almost swerved into this car beside her before it drove off. She chased it down on a short cut and swore and shook her finger at it, saying that the boys were "little" and "young" and "naive," but they drove on as if she were just another posted sign and the moment had not happened. Selma hates that they didn't scare her through sexual threat. Because Selma sits with Leonard and others and looks at this little boy during mid-day on a Tuesday on the Southside, and this kid reminds Selma of the bandits in a Chevy amid the woods in the U.P. All she can understand is that it is about being on the other side of the fence. Here she sits, longhaired still, and this fellow cares about her nametag. He looks at the others sitting in chairs, in the parking lot contained by the fence, and she wants to know why it isn't Her hair or Her skin or Her age that could have captured his eye. Enough so that her friends wouldn't have been made to bother, enough so that she wouldn't have said, "them." But Selma knows this parking lot is vast. And she is no longer on a full ride.

My father and I were bent groundward and picking up pebbles while arguing in our confused, disconnected way, when from up above and behind us the sword of Hephaestus swung down mercilessly to slice my father all the way plumb from his asshole through to his left hip. Then for a second go it came back around, back into the asshole and down through the groin to sever his left leg completely. The sword of Hephaestus was forged of a bronze and silver hybrid that changed color from bronze to silver to blinding in the light. It was lean and strong, and handled effortlessly as it whipped through my father's ass.

Before disengaging itself from his body, my father's left leg shivered a bit, then plopped over and into the sand. From his pelvis, blood sprayed in an arced line, like water from an oscillating sprinkler. I rushed towards him, sorry for all I had said, and intending to offer support before he lost balance completely. As I ran I saw with horror from the corner of my bulging, terrified eyeball that the sword of Hephaestus was now swinging straight towards me. There was no getting away: I knew this, and flinched. The sword of Hephaestus caught me between the thighs and sliced off my right leg, easy. The blade took an abrupt swerve then, the flat side slapping my ass before striking the ground and rescinding into an overcast sky.

As you might guess, we both hopped around screaming while blood gushed out of our hip joints and clotted the sand into crimson lumps. Having always been the more competent in times of crisis, I bent down, wincing at the pain in my sliced socket, and picked up my father's left leg and my right leg, respectively. I ordered my father to walk west along the river. I linked my arm with his and we managed to pogo together, like the elementary school field-day game where you tie your right leg to somebody else's left leg and become a three-legged creature, only we had no third leg to share. All the while, my father wouldn't look at me, not even a sideways glance. I spent the time wondering what Hephaestus had meant by such a mean swipe; he of all the gods seemed most likely to be sympathetic. In silence, we continued to take generous hops by turn, our remaining legs strong as steel, as we advanced towards the closest hospital, where the doctors stitched us back up, saying we were lucky he didn't slice through our hearts.

I guess we weren't supposed to have gone to the hospital, because it made things a lot worse for us in the long run. A few hours after arriving back home, where my mother stirred spaghetti in a strong steel pot, I felt a strange rumbling in my hip socket precisely where my leg had been stitched back on. My father expressed feeling a similar quake in the middle of his left pelvis. That was when I knew we were to bear immortal children from our wounds. I quickly unlaced my stitches and pulled off my leg, allowing a full-grown god named Meninges to spring out, panting heavily; he had almost suffocated in there. My father did the same with his stitches, and from his pelvis leapt a beautiful goddess named Hysteria, with golden locks, coral lips, and the rest.

Hysteria and Meninges immediately embraced, ignoring their injured parents. My father and I stitched ourselves back up; it's not hard once there are holes to guide you. Looking at one another, we each saw our children's mythologies in the other's face. They would love each other, grow old together, despite/because of having an unusual sex life and an uncommonly high number of shared genes.

It has been difficult knowing my son's father is also my sister's father: it's like in the movie *Chinatown*, with the difference being obvious. For me, this has all been a small if unusually sharp bump in the proverbial road of life; for my father, it has been a wall. He walks now with an imagined limp; his head, shoulders, knees, and toes all drag, increasingly lifeless as the years proceed. But my father has always been a homophobe. The knowledge that his immortal child was born with the sword of another man, and the ugliest of gods to boot, is simply too humiliating. This is what we had been arguing about in the first place: why I was so unfeminine, and couldn't I be normal. I had said I don't like being penetrated. He had claimed to dislike it as well.

We have never much talked about our experience with Hephaestus. It is the elephant in the room, as you can imagine. It's discomfiting to have these scars, like matching tattoos, marking the history of what we most wish we had not been through together. Otherwise we're not very close, which I've always thought a shame. We're alike in so many ways.

William sat by the dry reflecting pool and ate his bagel without Justin. Here they would sit on a Sunday, after a long night of blowjobs and iTunes. William poked extra cream-cheese out the bagel's hole, letting it fall to the concrete. Like all city parks, Rittenhouse Square idealizes the nature everyone is missing out on, William would say to Justin. It's a biblical fantasy. Parks make trees a fetish thing. But Justin's thoughts would be lost in the refection pool, then full, approving how his eyes and nose and mouth made aesthetic sense together, while the faces of other park-goers seemed genetically slapped together, mutated into adult finality.

In Anatomy, William and his group were given a dead body. The hardest part to saw apart was the teeth. William let the girls do that part. It was an old woman's body and having never seen one in real life, he was unprepared for the intricacy of a vagina. So intricate! he exclaimed, poking it with the forceps. The skin is divided into folds, lying between the legs like a lizard in the sun, William wrote in his notebook. It feels as though the lizard hasn't moved in hours, but might at any second, slowly shift its weight. William nudged closer for a better look. He pushed his rubber-gloved finger against the vagina. The other boy in the group raised his eyebrows at William, implying. William snidely informed him that he was gay. The boy looked at him. William said something in a gay-sounding voice that made the girls smile. Then the boy moved closer to William and the vagina. "Well, usually this part is way more pink, and its sort of wet over here, like with an oil or shine or something." The girls squirmed as he described this.

At Woody's the dance floor was crowded with muscle-flexers, as usual. William danced near a cute boy with glasses. An older unattractive man danced towards William. In a series of moves, William escaped from the unattractive man. He danced up to the cute boy with glasses, but the cute boy danced into the center of the floor. William's dancing slowed as muscle-flexers filled the spot abandoned by the cute boy. Drunk leaving Woody's, he tripped on the pavement. Blood ran up to the surface of his scraped knees. William knew that in humans, oxygenated blood was bright red. He knew that deoxygenated blood was a darker shade of red. Also, there was a rare condition sulfhemoglobinemia that resulted in green blood, blah blah blah. He knew all about it. He looked at the blood on his knee and felt privileged to have his body. He didn't bother cleaning the dirt from the cuts.

Justin's homeless friend was sleeping in the doorway when William stumbled back to his apartment. William looked with interest at the man's slender arms. If the man was dead like in Anatomy, then William could touch the man's arm. The man woke up and looked at him, "Justin home?" he said. William wiped at his bleeding knees.

"Justin has left his home forever."

"Shame." The man put his fingers to his eyes, "He leave his anti-anxieties?"

"I don't know. I didn't check. Maybe. I don't know."

"He'd been giving me his anti-anxieties. Made him too dizzy." William studied the man. If he was the man, he would get more tattoos. Sometimes one looked lonely alone on an arm. William looked at a scratch on the man's knuckle. "Hey, that looks kind of infected."

"That so? You tell me, Medicine Man." William smirked and went inside.

✳ ✳ ✳

In the bathroom he brushed his teeth with his new natural toothpaste. As he sat on the toilet, he stared at the stupid inspirational poster Justin had left behind. *Learn to watch snails. Plant impossible gardens. Make little signs that say Yes! and post them all over your walls.* Yeah Right. William stayed up late looking at his diseases textbook, skimming for the strange and unusual. Black Hairy Tongue was a harmless condition sometimes caused by Pepto-Bismol.

William found himself on the website where he met Justin. Justin's profile still read the same. "I used to be religious. Turns out I just like mythology." William reread the whole thing, idly highlighting with the cursor. "My hair often has its own ideas about how it wants to be styled." Some sentences in the profile rang false, "I often have dark circles under my eyes because I love to sleep." Also, "I am a cross between Angelina Jolie and young Robert De Niro." Yeah Right. Then he highlighted what he hated, "You could spend a lifetime with me and never get to know every facet of my personality, though you'd have a great time trying." That was not true. William highlighted the whole thing blue, then unhighlighted. He considered starting up a fake profile and using it to flirt with Justin. Only if things got boring. Or stressful. If things got so boring or stressful that William felt suicidal, then he would instead start up this fake profile. As a gift to himself. And maybe also if he got slightly suicidal, he might let Justin's cute homeless friend live with him, because the apartment was so big and lonely, plus it would be a good deed!

* * *

Then it was the semester when William and his classmates were paired with different doctors. So far he'd had the dermatologist and the pediatrician. Tomorrow was the oncologist. William searched the medicine

cabinet looking for Justin's medicine and found bottles
and bottles of it. He gave some to Justin's homeless
friend and took some himself when he missed Justin.
Which was most times. He stared at his desktop back-
ground. He checked his knee and saw no infection. In
some ways, it was a shame. Once he had a staph-
infection and it was not an entirely bad experience. He
scrolled down his iTunes library, giving random ratings
to each song. When he came to his cousin's album, he
gave each song only one star, just to be mean.

On the day of the oncologist, William felt light-
headed, but it was just a side effect of the anti-anxieties. The oncologist poured coffee for him and William,
"It's good to make your patients wait a little, makes
them respect your time." The oncologist talked as they
walked to the first patient of the day. "Ms. Kespetrova's
situation is complicated by a breast implant procedure
10 years prior to the cancer." They strolled down the
hall side-by-side. "She has an accent." William kept up
the pace. "She's a real trip." The oncologist sighed,
fingering the cool metal part of his stethoscope. "This
is just for show," he joked to William as they walked
inside the room. Ms. Kespetrova sat in a fur coat on
the examination table. "I go half crazy in these rooms
waiting. Sometimes I go all the way crazy!" She smiled
at William. "That is what a doctor should look like!"
She nodded approvingly at William. The doctor spoke
to William about the left side tumor, showing the most
recent ultrasounds.

"I'm just a student," William explained and introduced himself. "I'm sorry to hear of your condition," he continued politely. The Russian woman laughed. "Do not be sorry!" The doctor looked uncomfortable. Ms. Kespetrova screamed, "I get to have it all!" She tugged her fur coat emphatically, "First no breasts, flat chest like a boy, then little tiny ones, then bigger and bigger, healthy full breasts, then bigger breasts for breastfeeding," she sighed, "then tired breasts, swollen nipples, sagging, then surgery and implants and bouncing breasts, and now lump, machines, x-rays. So much attention on my perfect breast and its imperfection, this one," she took off her fur coat and was topless. She shook her large left breast at William, "Soon this breast will be cut away. It will be trash in the bottom of a can. My chest will be lopsided, one-sided, original. My body is always changing." The doctor checked something in his cell phone. Ms. Kespetrova continued, "Aging does not necessarily have to be a disappointment. I had beautiful grey hair young, it made all the girls want to go and dye it like that. A girlfriend of mine, she had a humongous wedding ring. Diamond the size of a dinner mint. Once she was walking in Miami Beach late at night, a man on the street cut off her finger. At first, pain and despair, but now everyone admires her for it. She gave something up." William nodded encouragingly. The doctor shook his head. "We must be going now, Ms. Kespetrova, Dr. Muller will be in shortly." The doctor motioned to William and they went back into the hall.

"My wife wants me to pick up the kids, but there is no way I'll be out of here in time. The kids are at day care," the doctor said to William. "I need her to pick up the kids, or at least call the other parents to see if they will drive theirs and ours. I, in no way, have time to call the other parents."

* * *

Staring at the poster, William tried to think of a cool way to ask the homeless man to move in. He didn't want it to seem like a come on, but why would it seem like a come on? He smiled when he remembered the Russian woman. He knew just what she meant. Sometimes being sick is interesting. Cry during movies. Cultivate moods. He was going to have to destroy the poster. What had he been thinking before? The homeless man. Justin? Something about the woman. Like when he had his staph-infection, it was so gross and painful and horrifying at first. But then he got used to it and on medication and the pain lessened. He was no longer afraid of the infection; he was intrigued. His body had made something that needed him. He had to change its band-aid each night and check up on its progress. He had to care for it. Gently, he'd press the infection to ooze out pus. He liked thinking the pus was cum. Also, blood would come out, not dripping out, but in little balls. Balls of blood. Balls of cum. His body had made something for him.

The class had to write essays about the week with the different doctors. William's was titled "The Illness as Interesting Life Experience" and was returned to him with a failing grade. "Wha-at?" William asked the paper. His classmates were packing up their books. He ducked out of the classroom. He looked to see his thesis circled and question marked. 'In addition to sympathizing with the patient, the doctor can also treat the illness as an experience, as a creative capability of the body.' William rolled his eyes to himself. God, the medical world is so closed-minded. He started running instead of walking, crossing over to Center City in a hurry, sneaking onto 24th Street while the hand sign was blinking red. They're taking the body, a strange, unpredictable, wonderful mess, and they're boiling it down to a syllabus! William breathed in some car-exhaust. He stared at the mutant woman on Market St., her wig plastered to her head, her make-up like a voodoo mask stuck on from last year. Luckily, life can't be contained in a stupid fucking syllabus.

* * *

The homeless man cleaned up so nice, just as William had suspected. It was fun to show him the apartment. "This is Justin's mother's couch, but its mine now. It's ours," he said to include the homeless man. "It's yours," he said to be generous. "It pulls out." Together they pulled out the bed. It was nice to come home and find the man deep in reading the cookbook and the anatomy book. By now he claimed to have memorized the anatomy book.

* * *

Class was all review for final exams. William leaned back in his chair. Looking at the boys' bodies, he pretended they were corpses and he was to dissect them and re-sect them to form the perfect man. That was the FINAL EXAM. Then he would put the creature back to life like in Rocky Horror and have to successfully blow the creation to get an A. If the penis hadn't been correctly re-attached then an erection would be impossible. It would have Anthony's hair, Jake's full lips, Phil's arms, and Jennifer's eyes, if that was allowed, if he could take one thing from her. Maybe her eyes would mix everything up. The teacher scrawled study questions on the board. William had once heard someone describe a coma as the best rest of her life. Sign me up, he said to himself.

Once, after his wisdom teeth had been taken out, William had taken Oxy Contin and briefly gone into daydreams. The dreams were convincing. They'd have him in a scene with someone he knew and then someone would tell a joke, or share an idea, or nothing, then suddenly switch to a new scene. That was how William wanted to live life anyway, a little bit of this, a little bit of something totally different. Like if he didn't have to be one person the whole time. If he didn't have to drive from one place to the next, or need time to slowly take his mind off everything.

Sitting cozily in their living room, the homeless man quizzed William for the exam. William could only recall 3 of the 11 facial nerves. He thought that Lumber Puncture was when the spinal canal narrows and compresses the spinal cord, but that was Spinal Stenosis, said the homeless man. William didn't remember anything about the medial branches of the posterior divisions of the upper six thoracic nerves. "I haven't been having an easy time studying. The internet is soo distracting." He mixed up Mentencephalon and Myelencephalon. Whenever he heard Pancreas he thought about pancakes. "I've been dizzy. Studying makes me dizzy." William took a cigarette from the man's pack and got up. He took a piss in the bathroom, cultivate moods, ripped down the poster and went back to the living room.

"Your turn," he took the anatomy book and quizzed the homeless man. The Endocrine system was communication within the body using hormones made by the hypothalamus, pituary, pineal body, thyroid, parathyroids and adrenal glands. A sacrum consisted of five bones which were separate at birth, but later fused together into a solid structure. William wiped some sweat from his neck and smelled his hand. "Are you looking at the answer sheet over there?" William looked for a lighter.

"Answer sheet? This is my job application," he flashed the answer sheet at William. William looked up from his cigarette. He could see the homeless man looking flattering in slim-fit scrubs. The homeless man starring in Grey's Anatomy. He could see the 'Homeless to Famous' story being churned out of newspaper-making machines.

*＊＊

The homeless man scored William some painkillers like he'd wanted. He stood in William's doorway and tossed William the bottle. He scratched one arm with the other arm. One of these days William was going to lend him money to get another tattoo. The three-legged dog would look great with something completely different underneath it. Like a name with a date or something.

William signed onto the dating website as his fake name, Skyler. A boy had sent him a message. Bored, William scrolled down the boy's profile. His pictures showed him drunk on two different holidays, then once playing devil sticks in his living room. William took one of the Percocets, then went back to the computer. He looked at profiles for hours, "I was a Computer Science major at Temple, although I think I'm ultimately going to become a shaman of some sort," but then his eyes didn't want to do that anymore. He pushed his burning Powerbook from his lap. Running windows on a mac made him love the anonymity of windows. The gay dating site wasn't up to par. Like it left this aftertaste of disgust. Was that how dating sites worked? Was there a way around that?

William felt for his cell phone because there was a noise it had to make. For tomorrow, if he was going to wake up for the exam, then there was an important noise for the phone. A girl stuck her gum to a sign post and then walked down the street. William watched and remembered the drug. In a car, it was him and the homeless guy. The trees passed. The street passed. William was happy the drug was good at being a drug. Like what if the drug was good at being a food or looking good in a bottle, but bad at being a drug? Justin sat down, "You see I got this haircut, but it's making me hate myself." "I don't want you to hate yourself," William said, giggling. For some reason computers always asked if they should save files, when the files hadn't even been changed. It was a nervous habit of computers.

William sat with his uncle. "I wanted to see a bunch of little scenes. I wanted life to move fast, but I think its moving slow." His uncle nodded and said, "I mean that's why I moved away. It wasn't a right fit. Everyone looked at me strange because I was tall." William waited in line, "I thought it would be scenes." The wind blew each leaf on the tree. The clouds looked nothing like animals. His "Illness as Interesting" paper had made sense in the computer. All the letters were straight next to other letters. There was a lot to celebrate about having a body. Justin said, "Now we can talk about Skyler." William said, "Who?" William's Dad said, "Who?" In the dark, it was obvious again that William would not transform into a doctor, "That's alright, guys. We don't have to talk about me. We should talk about something important. We should talk about the election."

If the blood, for instance, got mixed up with some dirt. Then the body would start a war with the dirt, forming a pus wall to block the virus. The virus wants to live and then there's this conflict taking place within the body. William imagined an infection as a fly stuck in an egg yolk, as a bad smell traveling through a car window. A thing clinging on that didn't belong. Justin infecting the new york gay/queer/trans social scene. William infecting Upenn Med School.

The body can start sending out bad messages. The body can make things you don't want it to make. If there was class soon, then there was a phone that made it work. If the phone is by itself, then probably soon will not come until way later. The paper must've been in the completely utterly totally incorrect font. Many eyes wouldn't have been able to comprehend the font, maybe. Possibly, it was just a wrong font.

Then William was riding with the homeless man in a car. The homeless man drove quickly wavering in and out of the lines. From the passenger seat, William watched the windows, then the beautiful face of the homeless man. The homeless man was swerving. His eyes looked like he hadn't gone to sleep for the most of his life. The homeless man turned and said, "If you want me to drive, I could drive, you don't have to drive the whole way. I know you, you get tired." The homeless man drove on, gripping the wheel. He missed another line. He looked at William and said, "Man, your eyes look like you bought them used." The car drove half on the grass. A stick got stuck in the tire, then snapped. The homeless man looked at William, "I could just drive instead."

MICHAEL STEWART
SISTER

Part One

Chapter 1

Our sister is covered in glances. We watch her bud. We are aware of our sister sitting in her room. Our sister writes letters while she sits in her room. She covers her new breasts with thin pink bras some of which have embellishments, little flowers or hearts or other little things like that.

Chapter 2

She lies on her bed with large headphones clamped over her ears and her hair. Our sister likes bands and music and records and magnetic tapes. We bring these to her sometimes to see her smile. She soundlessly mouths the words of these songs, her tongue occasionally peeking out.

Chapter 3

Our sister hopes for a boy in a white coat to come to her window to enjoy how her breasts look in her little bras. We do not mind that our sister hopes for things like this. Sometimes one of us will dress in a big, thick white coat and go to the window and tap on it. But this is not what our sister hopes for.

Chapter 4

Our sister puts bees' wax on her lips. Our sister applies makeup to her eyes, lengthens her lashes. Our sister's cheeks are naturally flushed. This is because our sister brings the frost in with her. If she wishes to look at herself she must wipe the mist from the mirrors. Our sister fits inside of her room everyday a little less.

Chapter 5

We try to read the letters that our sister writes. We steal them from the mailbox and steam the envelopes open. Without exception we are teased with blank pages of thick paper. The paper is slightly pink, as if blushing. Sometimes we catch the scent of our sister's lotion on the edges of the pages. The addresses on the envelopes mean nothing to us. They are nonsense, just random numbers and hopeful sounding names. She does not bother putting postage on them, we are the ones who paste on ten-cent stamps and send the pages out.

Chapter 6

Our sister reads Stendhal. This is because our sister's bookcase is only full of books by Stendhal.

Chapter 7

Our sister's lotion smells of grapefruit. She wears little tank tops under her long-sleeved shirts and these often smell of grapefruit as well. We know this because we wash our sister's shirts when they need to be washed and sometime we bring them to our noses. We love our sister so much, we love the smell of our sister even when it is only on her little shirts.

Chapter 8

Our sister's window is unlocked. Sometimes she opens it and goes outside. We do not stop her. We walk behind her to see where our sister would like to go. Every few hundred yards we ask our sister if she would like us to carry her. Our sister, we say, you are too small for the cold. Your lips lose their flush and become scaly. But she makes as though she does not hear us.

Chapter 9

Our sister keeps her secrets in an over-large seashell. She folds the pages of her diary into long strips and threads them into the coils of the shell. When the shell is full these pages look like tentacles. We are very careful when we unfold the pages because the oil from our hands can damage the thin paper.

Chapter 10

Our sister's hair is curly and messy and dull and a little sticky in places. We have suggested to her several solutions. We have slipped into her toiletries creamy conditioners that you leave in your hair and egg-based shampoos, but she insist on rubbing her hair and scalp with a plain bar of soap. Sister, we say, birds will nest in such nasty hair.

Part Two

Chapter 11

Our sister is gone. We are of two minds about what to do about this. We think, on the one mind, that we should find traces of her and follow her to insure nothing harms her. On the other mind, we might stuff her pajamas with tissue and blankets and clamp headphones over the top. This way waiting for our sister will be less unpleasant.

Chapter 12

While stuffing her pajamas we debate how best to make the proper bumps. We settle on wetting the blankets and using one of our sister's bras as a mold. After we solve this problem then we must decide about the knees. We are inclined to make them too prominent or to forget them altogether.

Chapter 13

We assume she used the window, but never before has the creaking of the window opening failed to wake us. Still, what are the other possibilities? The front door (too brazen); the back door (non-existent); a tunnel (we have found no evidence of one). It must then be the window.

Chapter 14

Our sister has taken with her: a book of Stendhal, some green ribbon, her shell and a new pair of shoes. It is the shell that worries us. The shell implies that she means to take her time in returning.

Chapter 15

When she was young we gave our sister a digital watch. If you press your finger to its face the digits fade and smear. If you press a button on the side then the whole watch lights up in a pleasant way. Our sister has left this watch in her jewelry box.

Chapter 16

Our sister may have fallen in a hole. She may have been carried away by birds and taken to the top of a very large tree where she would be forced to make a nest out of her hair and to tie shiny objects onto the end of her ribbon and to use this to fish for magpies so that she might eat. She may have made her way to the sea and found a small boat moored in the silt. She might have dug a trench to set the boat loose and used her dress for a sail and now she could be sailing east (the wind is blowing to the east). Or she may be burning the pages of Stendhal to keep warn while she huddles under some freeway imagining the occasional sound of traffic are the sounds of the ocean and in this way try to lull herself into a tearless sleep.

Chapter 17

The lump that we have made into her likeness does not move its lips to music and is, when properly considered, uninteresting.

Chapter 18

We have looked back into our notes to retrieve the addresses that we had once found so fanciful. To each of these addresses we have sent the following message:

Sister,

We have littered your windowsill with treats. Magnetic tapes of radio programs that we know that you like to listen to. Chocolate truffles, which we have usually kept from you because they make your face red and bumpy, but which you sometimes sneak from the cupboard and hide in various places around your room. And a kite, watercolors, earrings. We have done this in the hope of attracting you, but so far we have attracted only ants, pecking birds and a cat.

We have included stamps and paper and a pen so that you can tell us if you will need a train or a ship to bring you back.

And we have signed it accordingly.

Adding at the end a little post-script: P.S. Sister we hope you are warm.

Chapter 19

Those fanciful addresses are the addresses of men. We have no proof, but we are expressing what we believe. Thick, rude fingered men. Men with small patches of stubble on their necks and on the edges of their chins even when they have just shaved. These men, let us be honest, our sister prefers to us. Who have grinned while they have touched our sister's little bras. Our sister has gone swimming in that terrible legion of men.

Chapter 20

We have recorded the following problems since our sister has left. Headaches, hair loss, sore fingers that throb in the cold, a loss of appetite, drowsiness. Sometimes we also have problems with erections.

Chapter 21

We send up bottle rockets and watch them bloom red and green, sometimes dusting the night with hot, white sparks. Each with a trail of smoke tethering it to our house. If our sister sees these perhaps she will see that we are having such fun here that she will want to join us. If our sister is lost, then every night, in two minute intervals, we will guide her back. We use only her favorite colors. On nights when it is raining and we cannot fire the fireworks we sometimes despair.

Part Three

Chapter 22

We have received an envelope. Inside are four blank and slightly pink pages with the smell of grapefruit tucked into the creases and the slightly shiny remnants of lotion where her fingers must have pressed to crease the page. But we cannot read those blank pages! We have tried heat, light and lemon juice. We have tilted the pages looking for the dull impression a pen might have left, the ghost of the words she would have had us find. But the pages, they are blank.

SEAN KILPATRICK
GANGRENE

1.
A pretzel on the side of the freeway,
or road kill, a dog hit by a car,
I thought it was my father for a minute.
The doctors came slowly out of their tents.
The passing cars almost touched their zippers.
One scratched and said, "we should operate."
"Hmm,
we don't want to say bladder infection just yet."

6.
My rifle fired embalming fluid into the sky.
Mascara sunset rained a coffin smell.
I told the doctors about lipstick.
I said my father's sad grins were populated
by formulas you could never memorize.
We decided to paint rouge on his coffin.

9.

Gary was sometimes my real name.

I found a mean stare in the garbage

and put it on for awhile.

I made a career out of following my kitchen with a
noose.

Flowers made of smegma ruined my lawn.

Gary shook his head.

With 10,000 volts, he shook his head.

16.

I was a chore of gangrene headaches.

Several thousand maggots watched me

through a magnifying glass.

I faked being wet for their entertainment.

I was convicted of drawing my own chalk outline.

Convicted of stealing my own chalk outline from the
Louvre.

1,000,000a.

Tawdry fucking yes all the way home.

Jesse Jackson won big at the circus.

For dinner, we found Jesus.

Told that sunset to shut right up.

2.

Neat breaks of ammo stung the weather.

They played my father's rigor mortis over the
loudspeaker.

Doctors with poor eyesight wearing rubber boots
through his carrion, with southern accents in his
   carrion,
on lunch break, the color of lotion, his carrion in
   tents,
said, "toothbrush removes father." They
said, "he served us well, your daddy pile
of Frogger super-genes gone splat."

5.
"A microbe of contorted dung.
Cerebellum of a dog whacked to lettuce.
Dead egg roll strap-on parent.
We'll save him with Bioplasty and good intentions.
Kiss musical gangrene with politics you deserve.
Make sure to swab his coffin with rouge.
A greeting card for the biohazard that came you
   here.
Applaud his temperature. Burn the ass a second
thermometer hole. We're on the smelly job.
Septic hieroglyph, STAT. Shake its hand, STAT."

11.
I told them I don't sing. I told them I don't do
   anything.
They wanted to roll me in mayonnaise until I talked.
I told them I self-reflected once.
Christ trifecta dreamgallow waltzed the fetish
into bigger, badder stoves than that.

I dreamed of noose-filled kitchens on purpose.
I had become a transvestite to get closer to mom.
Wearing pants was lonely. I laminated my first pair of
    pants.
I agreed (passive aggressively) to lecture
(a defense mechanism) about gangrene
(defined as) a nocturnal emission cornered by
    microphones.

18.
The white guilt prognosis, indicated by lack of sex
    drive.
The posse of corpse puddle or doctor
wanted my tongue for the evening news.
I was handed a legal document that said I had to sit
    down.

1,000,000b.
If we are in a room and you turn on
the television I might jump out of the room
and take the room with me.

4.
Their surgery lamp swung the rain at queer angles.
"We'll hide scabs in all your funeral roses.
Give us a smile, we insist. We need something to
    clean the port-a-potties with.
Do you see how the skin of this freeway is like
    gangrene?

Notice the unpleasant texture as I grate your face
   against it.
Never let me catch you putting lipstick on this
   freeway.
The cracks remind me of my daughter.
Did you know that some patients have been caught
trying to hide their gangrene under gobs of mascara?
But you always know who's gone putrid a second
before it happens because you smell the circulation
   stop
and when you touch her it's like Playdough in the
   microwave.
You've had your five minutes up my daughter,
cough her to me, toss her next to your shit smear
and we'll take a family portrait."

8.
"I admit Hitler's baby dick sauce rules my roost.
9-11 is the butter they found me in.
Goodbyes are my introduction.
You could say I'm an auditor of the uterus
or just plain a trough for the diarrhea of monkeys.
My parents dressed like tag team wrestlers when they
   beat me.
My parents dressed like Laurel and Hardy when they
   molested me.
'Doesn't that thing between your legs feel like an
   incomplete masterpiece?'
my father was fond of saying.

Nevertheless, scatological as it may sound,
he was like a father to me, my father.
We used a podium for our stains, oinked into
    garbage bags."

13.
Hereditary gangrene, compost DNA, born with
spinach headaches, that smell, maggots posing as a
    brain
treated my glands like dog food, until I bent in
    squalid
light and prayed for AIDS or anything to applaud.

19.
"When I say 'fuck you in the ass' I mean
you specifically and by that I mean whoever."
My mother was apologetic for failing to abort me.
"You can tell by the way I climb stairs."
Night of my first erection, I hoped the earth would
    die.
"You should have seen my lawn in those days.
By 'your wife,' I mean: genocide colanders of piss
or until stitches follow someone else's progress."

1,000,000c.
MC Hammer pants.
Vanilla Ice girlfriend haircuts dictate lingerie
    genealogy.
We tried once and lost our underwear.

We tried underwear once.
We lost our pelvis to good conditioners.
We had a bag of fat people tears
that we used like a telephone.
We were totally into public execution
before it was popular.

15.
We smoked the lake. The lake was too wet
to smoke. We smoked the lake. The lake was
    popular.
I came out holding a television. They charged me
    with rape.
I utilized a banjo. A roomful of traitors masturbated
    into a cup.
The pigment of your life was all I'd trained myself to
    wound.
They wiretapped our piss with too much adoration.

17.
It was regulation to breathe in the city.
If you refused, someone did it for you.
I held my breath so hard I ended up in the country.
You were standing there in the road with your fake
    signs
that made me love you.
I used to want to kill anyone who played guitar.
Before I met you, I used to want to kill
anyone who had small hands and I don't know why.

I'd still kill you, though.
You were going to ask for my green card
and I was going to show you the freeway
with dead toppings that called me son.
Instead, we pretended to fire each other from jobs
    we never had.

20.
I loved the color of your hair before
you signed it all away to undeserving charities.
I sent this fucked up letter about how you made my
    face
wet like birds, remember? You were Apple-Beak-Grin-
    Girl.
What kind of skewer did you call these arms
when they held someone who smelled like me?
I was executed by doctors because of poor
    metabolism.
When they pulled the trigger, my hair became pigtails.
"Beauty takes the grease you know."

1,000,000d.
A snifter of posh screams will make you itch.
A glob of telephone brings health.
Put me to sleep with enemas of snow.
Snow my pox until skin doesn't happen.
Beauty takes the grease you know.

ANDREA KNEELAND
IF I WERE LEE'S GIRLFRIEND,
I WOULDN'T WANT TO DROWN
CHILDREN IN THE DUCK POND

The down of its breast is the same color as a cantaloupe and fuzzy like a tennis ball. Its wings look like pale soot. It falls over, stands up, collides with a peafowl, tumbles down again in a shock of vertigo. All of the other birds fan away from the damage calmly, their dusty brown feathers soft as baby skin. They're kind in their ignorance.

My research partner records something in her notebook, bites a ham sandwich.

As for me, I am a little concerned that in the spot where I should feel guilt about Lee's girlfriend, there is nothing but a muted hope that she will just sort of disappear.

My partner erases something, mashes white bread into the cracks of her teeth. The bird has fallen again; its legs whisk through the air in a precious little fury. We sit and watch.

The thing is, I say to my partner, the thing is that he's going to forget all about how much he likes me while he's in Bermuda. I already know that.

She writes something else down in her notebook, or maybe she draws a picture of the bird's terrible spinning claws, with squiggles around them to indicate motion. If I were my partner, I would burn all of my notebooks after submitting my reports. They reek of subjectivity.

The thing is, I say to my partner, he'll remember how much he loves his girlfriend while he's in Bermuda and he'll forget all the promises he made while he was fingering me in the back of his car. I already know that.

The thing is, he'll feel guilty.

I stand up from the picnic bench and nearly knock over a toddler. It has whiteblonde hair and watery little eyes and I almost double back to knock it over on purpose but then I realize that

A) the toddler has nothing to do with Bermuda

B) knocking over a toddler, coupled with all of the other petty things I've done this month would be enough to make me a bad person [stealing my grandmother's arthritis medication] [purchasing those ugly Givenchy shoes for $570] [feeding alka seltzer to squirrels]

C) the toddler's mom might be watching.

Instead of knocking the kid over, I keep walking and instead of thinking about how I will never have a baby with anyone I want to have a baby with, I think about how I don't want to have a baby at all and I fantasize about torching all of the strollers and pushing the mothers head first into the flames. Then I remember that strollers are flame retardant. I wonder if I kept a flame thrower aimed at a stroller long enough, whether it would set fire or just melt. In any case, the kid inside probably wouldn't do too well.

If I leave them in the strollers without setting anything on fire, they still won't do too well. That baby has three times more neurotoxins in its system than I do, just because someone is afraid I might torch the stroller with a flame thrower.

This is hilarious.

I wish we didn't have to do research in the park.

Birds should stop hanging out in parks.

I hate the duck pond and want to drown all the children there.

I pick up the fallen bird and return to the picnic bench where my partner is gutting the ham sandwich, extracting mustardy slices of meat with her fingertips. She drops the bread on the ground, creates a cluster of pigeons. I think that they're real.

I set my bird on the picnic table. Its eyes look like inky wet pools from far away, but close up they are prismatic, made out of a thin black material that reminds me of the tape used in old cassettes. I imagine sticking a needle into the tiny socket and drawing a thin strip of blackbrown tape out, unrolling it onto the pavement until it flickers against the sun.

When I was a kid, nothing was prettier than a broken cassette tape on the road, its innards all unrolled and shiny.

That's not true. I didn't think anything about it when I was a kid but I remember it now.

The thing is, I say, the things is, I am not so interested in forgiveness. I just want to win.

How can you win? she says, This is not a competition. He has a girlfriend. She reaches out to stroke the bird's wing. It twitches.

A seam runs straight up down the bird's chest. Up through the beak, down between the legs. I slide my fingers along the ridge, feeling beneath the feathers where the two sides are joined together. It was a cheap mold.

The thing is, I say, but I say this to myself, not to my partner, and I think it instead of saying it. The thing is, if you recount the things that happened not as you remember them but as how they happened then you are perceived not as dishonest but as untruthful because how could a person be concerned with truth if they are not concerned enough to make it their own: how can trust exist in that void of sterile memory?

I turn to my partner and tell her that he said he would call me every day while he was gone.

How could he call you every day? she says. He's in Bermuda.

She pauses.

With his girlfriend, she says.

I use a tiny scalpel to make a slit in the bird's skin and I peel the flesh back until I can see the plasticky joints that hold the crude seam together. Its legs are still spinning. It's hard for me to believe that none of this hurts.

What you're doing is wrong, she says.

But he promised, I say. Which is such a stupid thing to say that my partner ignores me, even though she's finished the ham sandwich and has no other way to occupy her mouth besides talking to me.

Sometimes you can't tell if it's real or not until you slice it open and find your hands covered in blood.

The joints are cheap and don't want to budge. This is like unbuilding furniture from Ikea: nearly impossible without breaking something important. I slide my fingernail into the joint, wiggle it gently. A tiny little talon scrapes against my wrist.

Where did this come from? I say.

China, she says.

That's not what I mean. The joints finally unhinge. There is no blood. The innards shine like jewels.

I don't know where to begin.

They call us researchers, but it's just a title: I make the same money as a receptionist or a girl at a make-up counter. We are not researching so much as documenting, and we are not documenting so much as troubleshooting imitation wildlife.

I mean which company made this one, I say, even

though this is what I'm supposed to figure out. If you could tell which company made the bird just by looking at it, then I wouldn't have a job.

I avert my eyes from the gleam of the bird's cavity and watch a little girl with a french braid. She has glasses strapped to her head with a wide pink band of elastic. She plops herself on the muddy wet grass, digs her hand into the ground and then shoves a fistful of earth into her mouth.

I open my tool kit and remove a vial and a Q-tip. I pour a few drops of solution on the Q-tip, rub it against the bird's liver, then stick the Q-tip into the vial and wait. The Q-tip turns black. I pull another Q-tip and vial from my toolkit.

I don't understand why we have to test every organ, I say. If the bird's made out of lead, then the bird's made out of lead.

My partner shrugs her shoulders. Specificity, she says. She's drawing a picture of the bird's heart inside her notebook. Inside of the heart, she writes "LEAD" in big bubble letters. The heart is made out of copper, I say, but she doesn't fix her drawing.

I told him, I say, that I don't want to be the other woman.

And he told you that he wasn't going to leave his girlfriend, she said.

But then he kept calling me anyway, I say. And I kept telling him that if he didn't want to leave his girlfriend, he shouldn't be calling me. I seal 3 vials of blackened Q-tips inside a ziplock bag.

But still, he kept calling me, I say.

She's drawing cartoons of internal organs. She ignores me.

I don't know why people mistake bluntness for invulnerability.

Sometimes I think I should orchestrate train wrecks for a living. I bet the job actually exists out there, somewhere. In Hollywood.

Or Bollywood.

I wouldn't be very good at the pyrotechnics portion of it, but so far as the general concept and layout, I would excel.

I am a big picture person.

Excuse me, I say, and I walk to the public restroom. I close the door, waiting to cry. I think about Lee. I think about kids in Guangdong province, hunched over melting hard drives and printers and cellular phones. I think about Bachna Ae Haseeno, which was a such great movie. I think about egrets and chickadees and hummingbirds. I think about the extinction of the species. I think about machines. I get distracted by the filthiness of the toilet and the wetness on the floor. I think about my massive credit card debt and the $400 purse I ordered from Bloomingdales.com last night. Nothing happens. I think about what to have for dinner. I open the door and stare at my blank nothing face in the mirror, disgusted.

My partner isn't sitting at the picnic table anymore.

She's crouched down, talking to a little boy in corduroy overalls. Her tennis shoes are sunk deep into the sandbox. Those shoes are going to reek of dried piss.

I pick up a rock and toss it into the pond without any illusion of grace. It fails to make a significant ripple; the ducks continue to ignore me and go about their business.

If this were a Bollywood movie, Vishnu and Lee and my dead grandfather would rise out of the water. The birds would ascend in impossible brilliance. We would all climb to the top of the train and dance into a hallucinogenic explosion of fireworks and rose petals.

Kids are screaming, lobbing whole slices of white bread at a mallard. I can't be certain whether or not it's real. I think about the different ways I can try to make it bleed.

DEAREST AXELHANDS,

(1) YOU DON'T NUMBER LETTERS. I AM WRITING FROM THE ARIZONA DAWN. THE BIRDS OUTSIDE ARE EATING EACH OTHER ALIVE. AT LEAST I HAVE NOT OPENED MY EYES TO FIND MYSELF ON THE ROOF OF A SALON, STARRING UP AT A CONSTELLATION OF THE SEA, CHOKING ON PEPPER EGGS. THE BROCHURE FROM THE FOREIGN OFFICE DEPICTED US THERE, WATCHING THE LAVA FROM THE STARBOARD SIDE. 'YOU'RE A BORED AGAIN VIRGIN' THE FOGHORNS JOKED. ARE CATS MORE ATTACHED TO PEOPLE OR PLACES? PERHAPS YOU'VE ALREADY NOTICED THE ALTERNATE SPELLING OF THE WORD 'FLAVOR', OR MAYBE YOU ARE FAMILIAR WITH SAINSBURY'S FOOD STORES, BUT I'M KEEPING NO SECRET: SAINSBURY'S GENERIC BRAND BACON CRISPIES BACON-FLAVOUR MAIZE SNACKS ARE A DELICIOUS AND DIFFICULT-TO-PROCURE ITEM FROM OUR SISTER CITY, BIRMINGHAM. MAGIC IS THE ONLY REAL. WHEN WE RETURN I'M SENDING YOU THIS LETTER. IN IT I WILL SPEAK OF THE HEART. I WILL SPEAK OF CHILDHOOD CHICKENS AND THE MANY PATTERNS I'VE FAILED TO MAP ONTO MY OWN LIFE, WHICH SEEMS NOW DRAWN AS A SWORD, AND DULL AS A BABY, SOMEWHERE OUT IN WHAT IS NOW THE GREATER SOUTHWEST SEA.

WE CIRCLED, WILDCATS IN TRIPLICATE, NOSTRILS OUT, EYES DOWN. I CLOSED MY OWN, AND SAW THEM AGAINST A MYRIAD OF PAINTED BACKDROPS: RAGGED GULF COAST POST-STORM, DEEP-SEA CABIN HALF-EATEN, SMILING BY THE STEAM LINER, ALWAYS SUN-BATHED CHILDREN. GOLDEN, THEIR ARMS-WRAPPED AROUND ONE ANOTHER, STARING OUT, INTO THE WORLD'S BEDROOMS, HEAVY LIDDED. I'VE READ THE NEWSPAPERS HERE. THEY BUILT THE OLD ROAD FROM THE FLOORBOARDS OF THE BEACH HOUSE. IN FACT, THE PACKET (AS THEY WOULD CALL IT) CURRENTLY UNDER MY NOSE WAS ONE OF EIGHT — MINUS SIX EATEN BY HER SISTER, PRE-FLIGHT — SMUGGLED BACK TO THESE UNITED STATES BY THE TWINS, WHOM YOU KNOW. ~~AMOUNG~~ AMONG CHOCOLATE DIGESTIVES AND BEANS-ON-TOAST, BACON CRISPIES IS ONE OF THE FEW FOODS FROM THAT UNITED KINGDOM I WOULD DESCRIBE AS EDIBLE. WHEN THE BUILDING EVAPORATED I SENT THIS LETTER INTO THE HEART OF THE NIGHT, AND WE DECAMPED INTO THE DARKNESS, OUR BRAINS MASHED, THE STARS OUT IN PERCENTAGE. THE AIR SURROUNDING MY BODY WAS THE SAME TEMPERATURE AS MY SKIN AND I FELT NOTHING. I WAS TRYING TO SPEAK BRAZENLY ABOUT THE SERIOUSNESS THAT COMES IN THE SLEEP OF THE CHICKENHAWK. THE FACTORY'S RAFTERS KEPT INTERRUPTING AND I BEGAN TO SUSPECT I WAS A FLAW IN A PLAN I HAD NOT DESIGNED.

③ BACON CRISPIES ARE RECTANGULAR ~~CRISPS~~ CHIPS WITH BROWN AND RED STRIPES APPROXIMATING THE APPEARANCE OF SMALL STRIPS OF BACON. THEY TASTE EXACTLY LIKE BACON. I'M GOING TO START OVER.

~~DEAREST AXEL HANDS,~~ ~~DEAREST ALBIE~~

DEAREST JACKKNIFE PONDEROSA,

THIS DOESN'T SEEM TO BE GOING WELL. WHEN A WORK OF ART IS ABOUT FAILURE BUT FAILS COMPLETELY AT ELICITING THE SORT OF EMOTION IT WAS MEANT TO, IT GIVES BIRTH TO A CERTAIN TENDERNESS IN MY HEART. AN INCREDIBLY SAD FAILURE MADE ALL THE SADDER BY IT'S FAILURE AT SADNESS. YOU KNOW, LIKE RICK MOODY'S FIRST NOVEL, OR THE GIN BLOSSOMS, OR THAT MOVIE "SIDEWAYS". I'M STUPID. LET'S MOVE ON. FUCK THE FLASH IN THE BACK OF THE CRANE'S EYES. I'M WRITING THIS ON A ROOF. I'M MAILING IT IN THE MORNING. IT'S ABOUT MY HEART. WHICH HAS ONE HAND ON THIS DRINK. I HAVE BEEN APPOINTED AMBASSADOR OF ALCOHOL. THIS IS SERIOUS. I'M NOT JUST JK'IN YA. THE WAY THIS DRINK DROWNS IN MY SORROWS, BLANKED FOR A COUPLE BILLION BALLS OF TURNING GAS, STRANDED OUT UNDER THE "ALL WE CAN KNOW IS THAT I AM ALONE..."

(4) I'M TRYING TOO HARD. LIKE AN OLD JOKE. LIKE A COMMERCIAL. DUE TO GREASINESS AND CONSIDERABLE EXPENSE, FOUR OR FIVE STRIPS IS ABOUT ALL I CAN STOMACH WHEN IT COMES TO REAL BACON. AT A PRICE OF ~~50 PENCE~~ 88 CENTS FOR ~~100 GRAMS~~ 3.53 OUNCES, BACON CRISPIES ESSENTIALLY ALLOW ME TO CONSUME AN ENTIRE BAG OF BACON. CHEAPLY, AND STOMACH-ACHE FREE. I WOULDN'T WIND YOU UP. THE TWINS ARE DEAD. THEY DIED. HAVE I TOLD YOU? BOTH OF THEM. LOOKING AT THEIR EMPTY BODIES, ENTWINED, I THOUGHT TO MYSELF: MAYBE THEY ALWAYS WERE. DEAD, I MEAN. MAYBE I HAVE BEEN LYING, SAYING THEY ARE ALIVE, PRETENDING ABOUT SUMMER AND FATE AND THE ROOF AND ALL THAT. MAYBE THAT IS THE NEWS MY HEART IS MEANT TO FIT. AN ASTRONAUT, AGAINST A STAR FIELD, OPENING ANOTHER LONELY PACKET OF DEHYDRATED ICE CREAM. HIS EYES LIKE SNOWCAPS IN REVERSE. OTHER NEWS? THERE'S A BLIZZARD OUT, I CALL HIM RUSTY. I HATE REPEATING MYSELF. HISTORY HATES REPEATING MYSELF.

DEAREST AXELHANDS,

I LOVE YOU LIKE A SISTER.

⑤ I GUESS WE'RE BOTH STILL ALIVE. WHAT IS IT CALLED IF YOU THINK YOU MIGHT HAVE HYPOCHONDRIA BUT REALLY YOU DON'T? I'M WORRIED THAT'S WHAT I HAVE. STUPID MAGIC. NOT REAL, REAL LIKE THE SCREAMS OF COYOTES. DID YOU KNOW THEY SOUND JUST LIKE LITTLE GIRLS, OUT THERE IN THE OCEAN, DYING? LIKE SPOOKED AND SCREAMING CHILDREN. THE TWINS WARNED ME NOT TO TELL YOU THAT IN ARIZONA. WHEN I WAS YOUNG, THERE, MY CRUSH, BETTINA, HER FOLKS HAD A SPLIT-LEVEL RANCHHOUSE, WE CAMPED A MILE AWAY, DROPPED SOME ACID. WE WERE UP ALL NIGHT, BOTHERING NO ONE, BLOWING BUBBLES. WHEN THE SUN ROSE, THE SCREAMS BEGAN. THEY CIRCLED IN ALL AROUND US. BETTINA RAN UP TO THE HOUSE AND LOOSED HER TWO BORDER COLLIES INTO THE DAWN. WE CHASED THOSE COYOTES OFF. I WENT RIGHT OVER THE EDGE OF THE CLIFF, LIKE IN THE CARTOONS, AND HUNG THERE FOR A MINUTE BEFORE PLUMMETING, EXCEPT I DIDN'T PLUMMET, I JUST WALKED BACK OVER THE SAME AIR, BACK ONTO THE CLIFF. SLOWLY, BECAUSE MY BACK HURT. THE DOCTOR TELLS ME I NEVER HAVE TO DO ACID AGAIN. HE HANDS ME THE PACKET OF BACON CRISPIES. ASSURES ME THAT THEY ARE SUITABLE FOR SPACE TRAVEL, GOOD FOR MY HEART. I TURN IT OVER AND SPIT. FLOODLIGHTS ON THE NIGHTJARS. LIKE WATER IN THE TAPEDECK. I KNOW HOW YOU DIE. I KNOW HOW THIS ENDS...

BETH COUTURE
FROM *FUR: AN AUTOBIOGRAPHY*

Birth

Mary's older sisters tell her she was a mistake. They say the nurses gave her to their mother as some kind of sick joke, and they threaten to take vials of her blood and mail them to zoologists to have them tested. Once their parents find out the truth, they say, they'll send her back and get the daughter they should have gotten in the first place. One with curly red hair and freckles, and maybe a dimple in her right cheek. Somebody like Shirley Temple if she'd had red hair, or that girl in the Pepsi commercials. "The cute one," they say. They show Mary photographs of herself as a baby, face and body covered in thick dark fur. Mary can't believe she was ever so small. She runs her fingers over the fur on her arms, rubs it against her face. In the photographs, her mother holds Mary up to the camera, feeds her, watches as Mary's father tickles the baby's feet. In at least one of them her mother is smiling.

Learning

The boys at school won't leave her alone, and to keep them from bothering her, Mary hits and bites at them every time they come near her. One day Richie Freeman gets too close and ends up with a broken nose and bites on his arm, and Mary is sent to the principal's office. Richie will have to get a tetanus shot, and he will never look at Mary again. When she passes him in the hallway, or even when someone mentions her, Richie will stare at the scars on his arm, will run his fingers over the bump on the bridge of his nose and won't say a word. At night he will dream about her, and call the dreams nightmares. Mary looks out the window while the principal talks to her. He tells her he will be calling her father to come get her and take her home for three days' suspension. She watches snow falling on the kids outside playing, their mouths open as they shout, showing red gums and sharp white teeth.

Gone

When Mary's mother left, she didn't tell any of them where she was going. She packed up her small car with as much as it could hold, told Mary and her sisters to be good, and drove away. Mary's father gets checks from her once in a while, but never anything else. The postmarks on the envelopes are never from the same place. Mary doesn't remember much about her mother, and so she looks at photographs to remind her. There is a garbage bag full of them in the garage, and she sits on the cold concrete floor digging through them, running her fingers over the faces—her own, her sisters', her mother's.

There is one photograph that Mary can't stand—it is one of her mother alone, standing in the driveway next to a wide blue car. She is laughing, head thrown back and eyes closed, and her hand rests on the roof of the car as if to support her. Her dark hair is under a blue scarf, but strands of it have escaped and brush against her face. It is winter—the sky is white behind her and all the trees are bare, and Mary's mother wears a cream-colored sweater and a heavy wool coat. Her pregnant belly strains against her clothes. If it weren't for this and the soft down covering her face and body, she could be a model in a catalogue. Mary thinks her mother is the loveliest thing she's ever seen. She has to hold herself back from scratching holes in the photograph, from tearing it apart completely.

Puberty

When Mary turns thirteen, her sisters decide to shave her. She tries to fight them, but they are bigger than her, and they force her to take off her clothes and get into the shower while they look for their father's Bic razor and shaving cream. Lula smears her with shaving cream while Mel wets the razor and begins to shave Mary, starting with her chest. Mary tries to cover her small breasts with her hands, but Lula bats them away. "I'm not going to cut off your little titties," she says. She has to go over some sections of fur two or three times before she gets it all, and the razor leaves little red bumps all over Mary's skin. Matted clumps of fur gather at her feet. It takes her sisters over an hour, and when they are done, the only hair left on Mary's body is on her head. The rest of her body is marble pale and shivering. When her sisters leave the bathroom, Mary stands in front of the bathroom mirror for hours trying to figure out her skin.

A Miracle

The next morning, the fur has returned, and it is healthier and more plentiful than ever before. Mary lies in bed and rolls from side to side, pleased with the way her body feels against the flannel sheets. She can hardly believe she was even shaved in the first place. There is no sign that she was ever hairless, that her sisters have ever touched her. She thinks she must have dreamed it, but she can smell Barbasol when she lifts her arms to stretch, and when she sniffs herself, it is stronger. When she showers, the smell of the shaving cream is washed away, and all that is left is her own warm, sweet smell. She stays in the shower until Mel bangs on the door and tells her to hurry up, then she dries off and puts on her favorite t-shirt and jeans, victorious.

The Doctor

Her sisters won't stop nagging her father to take Mary to a doctor. They say there must be some sort of hormonal imbalance, perhaps it's hereditary, and they have a right to know if there's something really wrong with her. They say their own children, if they ever have them, might be at risk. When this doesn't work, Lula tries a different tactic and says that Mary will be happier without all that hair covering her. She says a young girl needs to feel attractive and desirable in order to succeed. This is what her teacher told her. She tells their father that he is doing Mary a disservice by not trying to get her help. Mary overhears them talking, and she tries to tell her father that everything is fine, she doesn't need a doctor, but her sisters tell her not to be so stupid. Mary bares her teeth at them, holds back a growl.

At the doctor's office, Mary is given blood tests, urine tests, skin swabs, and laser treatments. The office is clean and white and quiet, and Mary likes sitting on the examination table so much that when it is time to leave, her father has to take her by the arm to get her to climb down. She kicks her feet against the table and tells him she wants to stay. They find nothing wrong with her—in fact, she is healthier than anyone else in her family. The doctor says that the fur will likely fall out as she gets older, that he firmly believes that soon Mary will live a perfectly normal life. Later, in bed, Mary

can't sleep without the light on. She keeps one hand
on the lamp all night.

Kiss

Mary watches her sisters dance with their friends at her fifteenth birthday party and eats a piece of chocolate cake with her fingers. She sits on the stairs where no one can see her, but no one even looks for her. Lula and Mel seem to be having a good time, and Mary is glad. Their father has never allowed them to have a party before. He comes into the living room every few minutes with sodas or potato chips, but he doesn't say anything to anyone. When it is time to open gifts, Mary has to come downstairs. She opens box after box and says "thank you" without looking closely at their contents. The kids don't pay much attention to her, because Lula talks so much. She laughs and crunches chips, talks with her mouth full. When Mary finishes with the last box, she hears a boy's voice telling her to look up. She does, and is blinded by the flash of a camera. When she can see again, the boy is walking toward her, and he hands her a developing Polaroid photograph. She watches as her face appears, first yellow and fuzzy, then darker and more defined. Her mouth is open slightly and her lips are pursed like she is getting ready to blow a kiss to the boy taking the picture. She looks surprised, but almost happy. After everyone goes home, Mary leaves her presents downstairs for her sisters to go through and takes the photograph with her to her bedroom. She scratches the words *First Kiss* on the back of it with her fingernail.

First Love

Mary's second night on the road, two cars stop, but when the drivers see her face, they pull away before she can get in the car. Finally, a middle-aged man in a Mazda stops. He doesn't say much, but he offers her a can of Coke and a cheese sandwich from a cooler on the backseat. Mary falls asleep, and when she wakes up the man has stopped the car on the side of the road and is stroking the fur on her leg. She can't see his face, but his touch is gentle. When he sees she is awake, he stops what he's doing and starts the car. "It's okay," Mary tells him and pulls her tank top up over her head. His hand is warm and moist on her shoulders and neck, and her back. He caresses her, and at one point he presses his face to her back and breathes in deeply. When it's over, the man starts the car again and drives until they reach a truck stop. He drops Mary off there after handing her a twenty dollar bill and two more cans of Coke. Mary thanks him for his kindness.

Traveling Companions

The first person who joins her is a giant, and he finds her at a gas station in Lansing, Michigan where she is eating her lunch and he has stopped to buy a pack of Camel Lights. When he says hello to her, she has to shield her eyes with her hand and look up, like she is trying to find a sparrow on a telephone line. He smiles and folds his body into itself so he can sit down next to her, and they talk until he has smoked all of his cigarettes.

In Milwaukee, Mary and the giant meet a man with tattoos of ghosts all over his body. He says they are the ghosts of all the people he has ever loved, and all the people he will love. Mary thinks the man will kill himself, but when she and the giant leave Milwaukee, he comes with them. They meet people in every city they come to, men with tattoos or missing limbs, giants, women with patterns of scars on their faces or muscles like men. They walk through Wisconsin, Iowa, Nebraska, Wyoming. Pretty soon, Mary can't tell her friends apart. She practices fitting names to faces whenever they speak to her, but after a while she gives up and calls all of them by the same name. None of them minds.

Family

There are six gorillas at the zoo—one huge black and silver one sitting on a flat red rock, and three smaller ones, two of them holding babies, walking around and preening each other. Mary can't stop staring at them. The really big one watches her for a while, and then comes over to where she is standing in front of the fence. He crouches there on all fours, knuckles in the dirt, with his head raised and his eyes directly on her. She knows if she waits long enough, he will talk to her. Any minute he'll open his mouth and speak. Pretty soon the others come up to crouch with him, and Mary and the gorillas watch each other for a long time. She doesn't know how long. They seem so intelligent, so like people somehow, with their wrinkled hands that clasp each other, their faces, their small dark eyes.

Traffic

Mary stays awake until nearly sunrise and listens to cars traveling down the highway. She can tell the colors of the cars based on their sound, and she makes note of how many of each color pass. She wonders why there are so many red ones. She watches the giant sleep, curled in his sleeping bag next to the beautiful girl in the Stetson, and feels her throat closing in on itself. It has been weeks since she began dreaming about him. Mary counts cars and awakening birds and the number of times the dog turns in its sleep, but by dawn she gives up. As she falls asleep she wonders where the red cars are going, if the men and women inside them have been driving all night just to get somewhere warm.

Correspondence

Mary writes letters to her sisters and mails them from mailboxes in neighborhoods she passes along her way. Dear Lula, she writes, have you talked to Dad recently? Are you married yet? And Dear Mel, I passed a building on fire yesterday. The smell reminded me of you. Her sisters never write her back, but Mary tells herself it's because she's always on the move and they can't find her. Sometimes she sends them packages—photographs of sidewalks and street vendors, postcards, bits of tree bark and ballpoint pens, and she always includes a card that says Love, Mary. Mary doesn't remember what her sisters look like, but she sees their faces in all the women she passes.

Rooms

Sometimes they stay in hotels. When it rains or snows, when they don't want to fight bums for space on the sidewalks, when one of them has made some money, they get a room in a place along the highway and bunk down for the night. The girl in the Stetson loves hotel rooms and always takes a bed for herself, but Mary and the giant would prefer to sleep outside. They make a show of rolling their eyes at the girl in the Stetson when she gets excited about a Days Inn or Highway 81 Motor Lodge, but Mary is the only one who is really impatient. The giant grins at the girl when she pouts at him and usually ends up sleeping next to her bed. The others don't care about sleeping, so they play on the furniture and flip channels on the TV all night. They always leave early in the morning before the housekeeper comes, two at a time so the desk clerk won't notice them. Before they go, Mary writes her name on a piece of paper and tucks it into the phonebook so anyone who finds it will know she's been there.

Swamp

In Mississippi, Mary and her friends visit a cypress swamp. They walk on a bridge built over the water, and throw pebbles in to try to rouse alligators. The giant swears he sees nostrils poking up from the murk, but none of the rest of them sees anything. The sweat on their faces shines, and Mary's fur is heavy and damp. The cloud of mosquitoes humming around them is so thick that she worries about breathing them in every time she inhales. The girl in the Stetson stops to take photographs of everything, and Mary walks ahead. No one tries to catch up with her, but every once in a while they yell something, or whistle, or make some other noise to get her attention. She turns around and smiles at them, and keeps walking.

When the trail ends, Mary is far ahead of her friends, so she waits for them to catch up. She watches dragonflies skim the water, and when she turns her head, there is a turtle next to her, resting on a rotting log. When her friends finally reach her, the girl in the Stetson and the giant are holding hands. He dangles her camera by its strap from one of his fingers. Mary turns away and looks at the water. She hears gurgling and splashing sounds, sounds of something choking or calling its mate, but she doesn't know where they come from.

Bodies

The giant and the girl in the Stetson have started having sex—most of the time at night, and Mary tries to lie down as far away from them as she can, but during the day sometimes, too, when the group has stopped to have lunch or to rest. They hold hands and walk side by side away from the group, or the giant picks the girl up and carries her into the bushes. They come out a little while later with twigs and leaves in their hair, red faced and smiling. The other women in the group tease the girl in the Stetson, giggling like high school girls and asking her if the giant is giant all over. She blushes and scratches the dog's ears, and won't look anyone in the eye.

Mary can't help but hear them most nights, even though she knows they try to be quiet, and even though she sleeps with her pillow crushed against her ears—the giant gasps and groans, and the girl yelps softly. The dog sleeps next to Mary now, his back against hers. Sometimes Mary falls asleep to the sounds the giant and the girl make, and she dreams that they are two wolves killing each other, teeth tearing at throats and claws scraping flesh raw. When she wakes up, she has to walk over to where the two are sleeping and make sure they are still whole.

MIKE YOUNG
THE AGE OF THE TIRE BOAT

You are not the lasting tar pits that's the tarpaulin at last. You who opened Skoal beside the craters and the bucks, who spent a lot of quarters on the Feather Falling slots, who opening the mayonnaise elected not to think of what you'd thought about in fever, near junipers, near feverish junipers and jumping, giving up on fording to jump among the rocks. Who carried sluices and train tickets. I left my sunglasses in your woodshed can I get them in the morning. You are not the morning when you waded on a shelled out Honda through the water that was cold. You are not the nickels that you licked atop the bridge, ear to the rails and the lash of the whistle, not too far above the crayoned hearts. You are not the paper mills or granite mines in which you punched, punched out, sucker punched, Kool-Aid punch and rum, slightly tipsy saying things about the rice.

You are not the dam that tucks the water in the lake. You are not the backhoe that my uncle drove. You are not the California poppies that my uncle drove in buckets to the lake. You are not endangered in the classic sense, but I saw you give the ointment to your cousin at the rink. I saw you in the snow outside the diner outside Dunsmuir, frying all the ham hock for the glugged of the 5, where you slept in the bathtub, in a red hat, in the white habit of a dream in December, munching on the radio, opening the Skoal, ferrying the truckers through the blame accorded snow. You are not Lyle Lovett come among his tenants with a lamp. You are not in all the boxing in the basement of the church, parched, fleas in your teeth. You are not the echinacea or the cancer. Now you're both. Congratulations. You are still the awesome handjob that you gave in Hunter's truck. But now you've been the mug shots of the teeth after the meth, been serenaded by "well, okay, I think I'll give myself another chance," been robbed with a hair dryer at AM-PM, been stabbed in the shoulder dealing cough syrup to fifth graders, been Ben when asked for your first name by cops, and also: Eduardo. You are not the Marlboros in transit on the sly, inside your older brother's coat, Wayne's parka, Skylar's Wayne, yeah, Tristina's Wayne, yeah, that Wayne, no, that way. I don't know officer; we're just skateboarders. Skate or die.

You are not dying. You are not relaxed. You left your sunglasses outside atop the swamp cooler in August, and now you've got a fever but I think you'll need a ladder. You left the cockroaches in the medicine cabinet. You left your spaghetti in the bathtub where you slept. You came across the Boy Scouts on their pews inside the woods, what for, hi there, to arrest the pews and burn the pews, gathering and burning all the pews, to cook your bacon, thank you. You are not the note we left appreciating God. You are not the tire swing abandoned in the winter. You are not the census that you answered very carefully: of the gold chink, of the sluices, near junipers, of the tar pits, with the cedarwood pianos and the Chesterfield aunts, in the Yreka bakery and other lonely palindromes, of the lye and Sudafed inside your mother's swollen warts, up in the newer casinos to uproot the holler, of the touched asleep in corduroy upon the courthouse steps. You are here to swear a kind of throat. You are saving all the names inside your plutocratic wrists. You are worshiping embarrassed all the dead and skanky dead. You are taking off your sunglasses in barns and doublewides. You are digging up the graves beside the cannery, looking for your sunglasses.

You are not the boxes of the bees tamed for the almonds. You are not the squirrel in the breaker room. You are not the soldier gone allergic to the sun, whispering it's bullshit to his daughter on the phone,

THE AGE OF THE TIRE BOAT

climbing up the marquee now to swallow all his shit. Nor all of the linoleum or menthol or asbestos. Babe is not the fairy lanterns, fiddlenecks, or thugs. I saw you in a shopping cart you'd duct-taped to the rails. With a frog inside your holster walking slowly in the rain. Down Feather River Boulevard. Down your sister's former name. If I go missing at the diner, then I stole a semi truck. You are not the God that we encouraged on the lake, nor the cataracts of lightning, water gone electric, all a clunky wish for death.

You are not the lack of ideology we chased just like a wedding dress. Man is this an accent or a train. Every whistle brays to a conductor's lonely wife. But is the whistle just itself, is just a pierce of pitch itself and is the landlord up? Someone tell the landlord that the whistle's faking it. Tell me why the lonely always worship all the trains. You are not the light which runs the length of all the rails. Which you are not and which is light that's lonely for a jack. Wheat thins and deer jerky, still embarrassed now to love to be convinced by all the prayers. I wrote AM-PM and Chevron on strips of fortune cookie paper and made you close your eyes and then I laid them on your tongue and then we fucked inside the bathtub then we threw it in the lake. You are not the stolen shit we tithed unto the lake. All you want to do is feel things. Beneath the snow. Babe is this a parking lot that came inside my mouth? You know the lady at the Salvation Army wouldn't sell me those sunglasses at first, she said they were her boyfriend's, he fled for the Ozarks in September with her Bluetooth, promising to steal her a motorcycle in Eureka Springs, maybe Jesus, the tall one, plaster of Paris, now smell those sunglasses and tell them that they're not my boyfriend's. You are not her boyfriend since you're not a snowman, right?

You are not your prescriptions or not predestination or not what you don't believe in just because you don't believe in it. You have gone to find the cure inside the granite mines and punched, slightly tipsy, saying all the beatific things about the rice. Now you've been caught scaling the dam, been left a bottle of Four Roses on the nightstand and a coupon for In-And-Out Burger, out in the morning, out in the poppies that my uncle drove in buckets to the lake. You are not the one who found your sunglasses inside the bathroom at the rink. You answered very carefully: I left the woodshed with an almond in my pocket, I did not draw my heart in crayon, I've never seen you before, fed you ham hock, or let you sleep beside me in the snow. You are not okay. You are hitching a ride on the green bridge wearing only a habit. You are serving all the drinks to every soldier going blind. If I cut you open, would I find the stolen throats? God doesn't care about the kittens in the SYSCO box. God isn't there on the Greyhound through the snow. God is not a fireman. We are not God's tattoos. No one sleeps beneath the train except the light. God will never cure himself of how the whistle doesn't stay. Hock all your tobacco on the pillow when you go. We're buried in the lake and touching just to last. The silt's between my fingers now and now it's in your teeth.

KATHLEEN ROONEY &
ELISA GABBERT
CITY WALK IV. IX. XII. XIV

CITY WALK IV

When Marisa's in the city, she says she "can breathe"
Alcohol is a disbiotic   It will cleanse you   Concrete
angels flank the bank building   Pictures of random
sexy people taken with my camera phone   Leaves
smeared into the sidewalk   Visible testament or in-
visible testament   I despise my defensiveness   Fine
rain falling from an apparently cloudless sky, typically
observed after sunset   We look small from up there
This year is a sense year   I hate my knees   Dulcetly,
dulcetly I trip in the street   Cities, I heard, make space
timely

CITY WALK IX

According to the graffiti   I have wasted my life   Vis-
á-vis is a loveseat   I want an adventure story running in tandem with the romantic comedy   Sunshot
verisimilitude adumbrating my fate   Metanarrative or
meganarrative   Either way, bright lines of distinction
distract me from choosing the correct path   Tête-á-
tête, vis-á-vis   When it's in my interest, I'm likely to
fabricate a history   How will I be undone & what will
undo me?   We romanticize regret, you know?   What
thought isn't an afterthought?   Soon we will cease to
save our daylight   The night people will reign

CITY WALK XII

Suddenly aware of being filmed   Under a witty sunset no one can see   The grand fantasyland of Co-
ney Island   Am I always under surveillance of the
sunset—its dust & chaos?   Are we getting any closer
to :-) x 100?   Centripetal or centrifugal, cabs spiral
out from the center of the city   In Hilbert space, all
is empty promiscuity   Happy screams cascading in
casual unison   A pivotal scene   Literally thousands
of photons, held in my hands   Infinitesimal intervals
chalked on the sidewalk   In photorealistic detail, I see
you everywhere, everyone   Requiring the use of my
outdoor voice

CITY WALK XIV

Vertigo, nausea, fatigue, malaise   solitur ambulando—
it is solved by walking   Watching your reflection in
the buildings   I don't even know all the area codes
Is that how I look, sideways?   Poise & counterpoise
Ignorance & ignominy   The light hits at a disorienting
tilt   A girl screams *I don't even know who you are!* to
no one I can see   Never having lived at a ½ address,
having seen a ghost   Rime is white ice   An eclipse
in a photo   Naufrage means shipwreck, but can also
mean ruin   Or a house with a name

JOSHUA COHEN
RIP OFF THE WINGS OF DRAG-
ONFLIES; VIRUS; ON LOCATION;
STILL LIFE WITH GRAPES;
FOUR ART PIECES; A CHINESE
FOLK TALE, AND THE CULTURE
OF POP ART; ANONYMOUS ANON-
YMOUS

Rip off the wings of dragonflies

Rip off the wings of dragonflies, take their "spines,"
their central lengths and a bit of paste, affix them
down noses, between the eyes, one per customer. *A
dream.*

Virus

One knee must always be higher than both elbows. Both feet should be kept on the ground (floor, bed).

Your mouth must be open. One finger of each hand must be bent, but only at one knuckle (each).

It should be three p.m. or later. And your hair must be long. One eye must constantly wink at the other (infected) person.

This might be the only way to contract the virus.

On Location

It is a common problem in our cities today — When you don't know you're in a movie that you're in.

The director yelled, Cut. I kept walking. He followed me down the street, asked me to back up a block and walk again. I obliged him, my mistake.

But no matter how many times I walked that block, no matter how many takes, he wasn't satisfied.

He said, Just do what you did. You were so much better before.

* * *

A security guard stands outside my building and won't let me in until they're finished filming in the lobby.
    Last week I was mugged of a Find the 9's lottery ticket and an expired credit card.
    If only he'd be here every night, not just when they're shooting.
    I lost the pass they gave me, too.
    I think he thinks he's protecting my building from me.

* * *

When they need to film a movie set in the city but a decade ago, there's a certain neighborhood to use. There are neighborhoods for every decade, for every year, for every month. The right cars on the street, the right house designs.

My apartment is very December 2006.

That's when my girlfriend left.

*** '

A woman so vain she wants to look good even for the surveillance cameras.

A guard who falls in love with the woman he sees only on security footage. He stockpiles the tapes at home, he never erases.

You. "Who have I seen you in?"

If we ever make a date to go to the movies and you're late I'll already be inside the theater, not facing the screen, though, but looking out, J, turned around, for you.

Still Life, with Grapes

I plucked all the grapes and ate them up and was
drunk. All that was left was a network of stems, the
bunch's tangle I tossed aside and stared at. It began
crawling toward me, the stems spiny, skeletal: from the
floor, back up to the table up its legs, the animated
mess like a hairy spider creeping up my chest and
onto my face, pop, pop, digging two nubs into my
grapelike eyes — rooting there, blinding me unblinking,
dark and still, for another's tasting.

Four Art Pieces

There once was an artist so great that none could tell whether he made paintings, or photographs. When stupid people asked — casually, at a cocktail reception — he would tell them he painted, and so they would flatter his talent. When the intelligent asked — the culturally active, or critics — he would tell them he took photographs, which answer would flatter not him, but them.

* * *

Looking back on the statuary that has survived from Antiquity, we could assume that the men and women (to say nothing of the gods and goddesses) of those earlier days lacked arms, or legs, and often heads or noses. Just as a future civilization, looking at our busts set atop our columns in the halls of the museum, might conclude that we possessed no bodies at all, that we were only heads set atop poles as if the expressionless victims of the cannibal of fame.

In a sense, they would be correct.

It would be better to be an amputee divinity than a disembodied brunette. Even the possible pasts have been set in stone.

* * *

Painting a portrait of an animal on that animal's hide (as in primitive painting, on deerskin), or with a brush made from that animal's hair (ermine), is like writing a book about paper: It would be better blank. Let the creature loose. Let it find its dark or tree.

* * *

An alternative: To turn our women into paintings of women (which is photography), and to turn our paintings of women — from Dutch girls to pink, triocular monsters — into women themselves, who walk and talk. Which would be intolerable, especially on trips to the museum...

Art exists to make life more beautiful. It does this by being inept.

A Chinese Folk Tale, and the Culture of Pop Art

A Chinese folk tale is told:

There once was a painter famed for having painted a magical moon, which waxed and waned. This moon of his was exhibited in the Royal Palace of the Forbidden City (Beijing). People would gather there, and ignore the real moon above them, to watch this painted moon go through the very same motions: filling then renewing itself, day after day, month after month...

It went on this way for years, interest steadily declining.

One day, which just happened to be the day of the new moon, when the painted moon's canvas was entirely black, a vandal (who was just a disaffected teenager) crept into the Museum — the Palace was now a Museum — and when the guard wasn't watching spraypainted a white circle in the middle of the black canvas, directly over where the moon would shine — where the new moon, in fact, was.

This instance of vandalism revived interest in the painting.

People would come from afar, and listen to a docent expound upon the meaning of such a white blob — or, more generously, white circle — centered on a canvas that was otherwise all black. When she'd tell them that underneath this a fantasy moon was actually waxing and waning, filling then falling dark all this time, the gathered museumgoers would hold their chins, smile, and nod (needless to say, *flash photography was not permitted*).

Anonymous Anonymous

I went to a meeting for those addicted to anonymity
— to the anonymity of meetings.

   When my turn came, I stood up and said, hello, my
name is Bloviatsky, and I am addicted to anonymity.

   They said, you're in the wrong meeting.

   You want the next room.

MATT BELL
JUMPMAN VS. THE APE

OPENING (CUT)SCENE

The ape takes your Pauline in its arms, and then it climbs up, up, up. It climbs something that is less a building and more the idea of a building. After several floors, it sets Pauline down and then stomps its feet until its massive weight causes the steel girders below to crack and shift. You watch and wait, and then you plot your own path up the wreckage, because even though you won't be going exactly the same way, you will most certainly be going up.

HEROIC QUALITIES

You can run and you can jump. That's it. Even worse, you are not any better at running and jumping than anyone else. The things you do to prove you're a hero, they're things anyone could be doing if they were in your shoes.

Look at you: You're nobody. So small, just a red cap and red overalls dashing up the steel. Just a would-be hero, still hiding behind a moustache.

DAMSEL IN DISTRESS

Yeah, yeah, you've seen it all before. So what makes this different?

Well, for starters, she's your damsel this time.

And no one—no man or ape—steals from you what is yours.

STRATEGY FOR THE FIRST STAGE OF THE QUEST

Run to the right and climb the first ladder as fast as possible. Avoid the fireballs sliding along the tower's base, then run up and to the left, leaping over the bar-rels rolling down the crooked beams. Climb and climb, and when you get close, ignore the ape and go for Pauline instead, then scream as it snatches her away when she's just inches from your outreached hands.

Do not be discouraged. Do not give up. Instead, follow them upward as they climb ever higher. Hurry, before the ape puts any more of this steel tower be-tween you and it, between you and her.

THE APE'S MOTIVATION

The ape used to belong to you, and maybe you mistreated it a bit. You called it names, fed it too little, worked it too hard. Made it carry too many beams or pipes or whatever it was you needed carried. Maybe you did a lot of things one way that you might have done another.

When Pauline asked you to be better to the ape, you refused her. It's just an animal, you said, refusing to listen to her pleas for mercy, patience, friendship.

The point is, you were kind of a dick to the damn ape. So what? That doesn't mean it can just steal your girlfriend whenever it wants.

WEAPON OF CHOICE

So it's not all jumping and running. There is also the hammer, perfect for smashing barrels, for stamping out fires. You swing the hammer until your arms ache, until your shoulders defy you to lift it even once more, and then you drop the thing and move on. It is not the weapon that brings the hero fame, but the other way around.

STRATEGY FOR THE SECOND STAGE OF THE QUEST

The layout of the tower changes as you climb, as new dangers take the place of those you've already defeated. The barrels are gone now, replaced by conveyor belts loaded with great tubs of concrete waiting to crush you. The belts change direction without notice, but you're quick and agile and you get around them, get over them. The ape runs ahead of you with Pauline still trapped in the crook of its arm. You wonder where it thinks it's going to go. You've come so far, and surely it must know you'll follow it to the very top if that's what it takes to win back your girl.

WHAT PAULINE SAID TO THE APE

Pauline was always nice to it. She was the one who soothed it when it got an infected tooth, the one who brushed its acre of hair when it was filthy. She used to coo at the ape, telling it what a pretty monkey it was. Dodging fireballs while trying not to fall off a ladder, you can't help but feel like this is at least a little bit her fault.

THE LADY'S THINGS

Pauline is now far above you, hidden from sight by the darkness, her voice overwhelmed by the bellowing of the ape. Still, there are signs she came this way in its arms: her purse, her umbrella, her hat, all dropped or discarded. You scoop them up, tuck them into your shirt or hang them from your belt, knowing you might yet lose them, might have to find them again before you reach her. You do your best, and you hope that Pauline sees.

STRATEGY FOR THE THIRD STAGE OF THE QUEST

The conveyor belts give way to a series of elevators, a sight you at first welcome as a change of pace, as a rest from the running and jumping. It doesn't take long to change your mind. The ape's passage has made a vertical labyrinth of the elevator shafts, and you have to scramble from platform to platform to keep moving up. Dodge the spring-weights and fireballs the ape sends down, then make the next leap, the next clawing grab for the opposite side. It is easier now than it was before, because you are becoming some new thing, some distilled essence, an entity sharpened and consumed by your quest and by the obstacles that stand in your way.

The person you were when you started this climb is not the person you are now and is not the person you will be when you finish it. You are changed in the struggle, and you wonder when you reach the top floor if you will be the only one. You wonder what new form the ape will have taken, and who your beautiful Pauline will have become. You are right to wonder, and also to worry.

AT SUCH GREAT HEIGHTS

The wind whips through your moustache. It's colder up here than it is on the ground, and louder too. You look down just once, five or ten or twenty floors above the street. It's a mistake, and you won't do it again. Instead, look up. Search for Pauline, for the flutter of her dress, your favorite, the one she once wore especially for you, that now maybe she wears for the ape instead.

Focus, and by doing so, stay alive just a little longer.

THE TIMER

How high are you when you first notice the sound, barely perceptible beneath everything else going on? Not high enough. The sound is the click clack of a clock ticking, moving toward something unknowable, but, like everything you've encountered so far, almost certainly fatal.

Reach into the breast pocket of your overalls and pull out your watch. Make a mistake: Believe the hands are moving backward, when in fact they are count-ing down, falling toward some number that can never be expressed on the face of a watch, never exactly reached with just its big hand and little hand and its twelve inadequate numbers.

You can stare as long as you like, but you will not come to a full understanding, not yet. You can only try to move faster, ignoring the mounting pain and frustration, can only hope that by doing so you might outrace whatever doom this is, ticking away in your pocket, tucked against the angry red fist of your heart.

STRATEGY FOR THE FOURTH STAGE OF THE QUEST

This is what you've been searching for: A final solution, laid out for you as a clear, achievable goal. Arrayed across the final three floors are eight giant rivets that must be removed, after which the ape will fall. Cocky now, it's placed Pauline above itself, at the very apex of the tower, on a platform separate from the one it stands upon.

She'll be safe there, you think, and then you realize that the ape believes the exact same thing. It thinks Pauline is safe from you. As if you're the one she wants to be protected from.

The ape bellows, motions you upward. It curls a lip, bares a tooth, clenches a fist. Beats it against its chest.

You know the ape would crush you in an instant, if you were to fight it, but of course you don't plan to face it so directly, don't plan to let it answer your insults with tooth and claw.

You hope. You pray. You continue upward.

So close now.

THE MALLEABLE UNIVERSE

You loosen the rivets on the platform and the ape falls, its howls mixing with the wind all the way down. You climb the remaining steel and take Pauline in your arms. Her eyes do not meet yours, but stay focused on the hole in the air left by her captor, by its fall to the ruin of concrete below. You tell her she's safe, but she demurs, shakes her head so slightly that you don't notice her disagreement soon enough.

You have something else to say, and so you push on, confessing your love, telling Pauline what you have failed to tell her so many times: that you would do anything for her, that this is just the beginning.

You wait for her to say the same thing in return, but she doesn't. Instead, with a look that could break your heart, she says, "Maybe next time," and then, in a flash you're back on the ground, and the ape has Pauline, and it's climbing up, up, up, all over again.

Everything is the same, except—

Look how fast the barrels are rolling. Look how much higher the building seems now.

Look at the time, and how little of it is left.

You must hurry, must climb, pursue, follow, become: Jumpman, destroyer of apes. Rescuer of damsels. Furious eyes beneath a red cap. Little legs pumping, churning, like two frames of animation endlessly repeating. Everything is so much harder now, but surely you can still win. You have to, for Pauline's sake.

Far above you, the stupid ape shrieks with delight, somehow still thinking it has you whipped.

THE LIMITS OF HEROISM

When all that was asked of you was one single feat—to climb this tower and cast down the traitorous ape—you knew you could do it. But repeating that same quest over and over is a completely different thing. Exhausted from the climbing, you begin to make mistakes. A barrel slams into you and spins you to the ground. A fireball burns you before you can leap away.

You pick up dozens of discarded hammers, swinging them over and over until you can feel their weight numbing your arms even after you cast them away, after each spirals downward to the ground below.

You keep trying, and eventually you again make it back to the top of the tower.

Again you defeat the ape, and again you gather Pauline in your arms.

Again, you fail to convince her, to make her take you back.

Again and again, you do these things, until finally you begin to fear that you cannot.

KILL SCREEN

The 22nd stage. The 117th screen. These are words you do not know and yet they govern the world you live in. A flaw in the creation of the universe means that there is less time than there should be to save Pauline and kill the ape. The tiny tick of your watch is now the loudest sound imaginable, and as it counts down to zero it dashes your hopes that this climb will be the last, that there could be a better end to this ridiculous parade of towers and apes. You've been led to the brink of salvation only to be forced into failure by this flaw. The people who made this place—who made you and the ape and Pauline—they never expected anyone to get this far. All the carpenters in the world, and then there is you, the one person capable of exceeding their expectations, their perceived limits of obsession and drive.

And yet, there is still defeat, still failure in spite of all your heroism.

Out of time, cast your gaze upward. Wonder, for the last time, what it is she thinks of you from where she is now: with the ape, perched high atop the parapets, the two of them finally freed, at this, the very end of all the world you've known.

OR, RESET.

ADAM GOOD
GUIDED WALKS

About		Method
Inspired by Buck Downs' "In Memory D. Thompson"...	1	Enter an environment
...in which he walked through a graveyard, making rubbings from language on the gravestones, guided by the language of the environment and the emergent forms...	2	Walk around
This was the first time I saw an improvisatory, material-based poetic practice in action. It hacked my mind; from that point on, everything in an environment was material to be manipulated.	3	Record/capture fragments of language, allowing yourself to be guided by both the material in the environment, and by the form that is emerging from it.
I began to "write" poems using this method; my first "guided walk" was through my students' SAT vocabulary exercises. As my creative practice has evolved, I have used this method as part of the foundation for working with any material, poetic, scientific, narrative, etc.	4	In this manifestation, record the results in a single column of a spreadsheet, with each fragment taking up a cell. When you do a new reading, record it in the next column of the spreadsheet. This will lend itself well to re-use, including improvisatory readings, or "meta-guided walks" through all the guided walks.

I began to wonder, what could this process be used for, beyond the creation of poems? Psychology? Cognitive science? An engine to create seeds for new semantic realities?	5	Each guided walk, and the collection of all guided walks, will become its own environment for exploration, and will thus serve as a kind of feedback/feedforward amplification system for the thoughts behind, and represented in, the language objects created.
See Buck's work here: http://www.fascicle.com/ issue02/poems/downs1. htm & here: http://buckdowns.com/or- dering-books/in-memory- d-thompson/	6	When reading the spreadsheet, be open to new and serendipitous formations emerging.

....a real adam good joint....

http://therealadamgood.com/

date	7/7/2008	1/5/2009	1/9/2009
envi-ron-ment	My Living Room + Joanna Newsom	Seed Salon: Steven Strogatz + Carlo Ratti	The Book Of Lies, ed. Richard Metzger
	this set of experiences	feedback of	the guardian
	each a	understanding	of the
	tunable, turnable	building the	moment
	context	city	leading
	potential	some way seems	the exceptions
	reader	like	in unexpected ways
	of those	gorgeous divergence	differenentiated
	dimensionally agnostic	systems of	in
	orders	systematic guess	complex
	in the fire	why doesn't	storytelling
	that is the	the node	one of the techniques
	vernacular	happen	that can
	of the sphere	in proportion	survive
	and its description	to the model?	us
	complete	non-linear	we store it
	sky	dynamic	in huge databanks
	of those borders	picture	on a painted surface
	if on a	processor	in non-local
	message	calculus of	phenomena
	strung or sung or	report	this link
	entered into	on top	achieves
	some	of "pure"	some
	how	ontology	case
	I was of a season	topology.	of
	to listen	believe	agent
	to	it or	access
	the complete chronicles	not	this portal
	of the search for	architecture	sealed
	the hidden point		and
	that answers		blasted and
	to the art		organized
	a lottery		in its
	if anything		place

1/10/2009	1/12/2009	1/14/2009
On Intelligence, Jeff Hawkins + Silence, John Cage	Cognitive Psychology and Its Implications	Meta-Guided Walk 1 (through Guided Walks 1-5)
experimental	the	the
pitch	activation	differentiated
-invariant	will spread	complex
form	from	telling
listening	these	
to it	sources	stored
a new grounding		in
mid	emanate	structure
-us	into	
structure	believing	arrived
update	form	at
when they	from	via
enter	lost	non-linear
tonality	sequence	reporting
by their		
similiarity	the	achieves
to past	conditional	some
patterns	modularity	sense
they	children	
are amazed		of
a streaming	spontaneous	the node
change	speech	
of input	in	and
directing	song	its weather
what is		
	of edge	an input
one	and	into
support	case	
to		an architecture
establish	the stage	processor
similar		
language	if the stage	an art
of objects		if anything

ANDREW FARKAS
THE COLONIZATION OF ROOM
313

"My dear fellow!...Be so good as to be a little more particular with your expressions."
                                          - Daniil Kharms
                        "What They Sell in the Shops These Days"

With a whoosh, or possibly a swoosh (depends on
your viewpoint, really) the door between rooms 311
and 312 banged open, knocking over the five inch
tall Sunsphere previously ensconced in the model of
World's Fair Park at the back of the room, sending it
(the Sunsphere) careening into the center, appearing
for a brief instance (or a long jiffy) as if it would land,
miraculously, defying all the laws of physics, baffling
the laboratory technicians and experimenters, confirm-
ing the believers' beliefs, confounding the skeptics,
amazing the general bystanders, yes, as if it would
land, miraculously, upright at what could be deemed
the nucleus of the room (if one were so poetically

and/or scientifically inclined)—but, at last, the replica fell to its side.

And just like the heat that came gushing from room 311, agitated on by an enormous noisy floor fan, the former inhabitants of 311 rushed into 312 full tilt, which means really fast because (if one is so inclined) things set to their highest tilt settings are...fast? No, that's not right. Things tilted forward move rapidly, much as if they were going down hill. Yeah, something like that. Only not that exactly. I think. Maybe...

The 311ers were so eager to rush into 312 because the 312ians were doing it all wrong...and because it was insufferably hot in 311, being pretty much just about exactly twenty degrees warmer (only don't quote me on that), and there weren't any windows and the door leading to the hallway was stuck closed on account of this guy or maybe this gal (I'm not sure which) had a great idea on how to prop the door open, it was a really spiffy new idea that was going to solve all the air circulation problems not only in the present but for years to come, it was the door-propping-open plan to end all door-propping-open plans, and when he or she was finished implementing the idea, the door was firmly closed, no one could make it budge a single inch—although I didn't personally measure to see how far the door could move, but I have it on rather good authority from a relatively reputable source that an inch was right out.

But the 312ians were...

Well, to best describe it, imagine a hypothetical reference point known as Right On. This point is where one ought to be, except that so many people should be there that one is not good enough to describe these theoretical beings, unless one assumes that one means everyone who wishes to be Right On. But one would assume that everyone would wish to be Right On, so who exactly is this one that doesn't wish to be Right On? Presumably the 312ians. For if you were to imagine a hypothetical point known as Right On, the 312ians were located at a point diametrically opposed to that hypothetical point, diametrically opposed to the hypothetical oneness of the rest of the world, which would put them...where, exactly? I'm not completely sure, but, according to the 311ers they, being the 312ians, were way off—which can be their reference point: Way Off, or the point diametrically opposed to Right On.

Being Way Off (hypothetically, anyhow), the 312ians needed someone, or, needing more than one, sometwo, somethree, somefour, sometwelve, someeightyseven, somemillion, someinfinityplustwo, or more coherently someones (which isn't a word, but then neither is fantabulishical), to show them how it was done; it being the right way, whereas the 312ians were going about it like that, which was all wrong. Says the leader...okay, maybe not the leader as it were, since the 311ers didn't have a leader per se (from the Latin per, meaning "over," and se, meaning "himself," which this person certainly wasn't), but some guy...well, maybe not even a guy...okay, one of the 311ers shouted:

"Over here it's being done all wrong!" which he or possibly she liked saying so much that s/he repeated it: "All wrong!" and again for extra dramatic emphasis, "All...wrong!"

As you might imagine, if you're prone to imagining things, and if you're not then you wouldn't imagine this either, but if you are then you might imagine that the 312ians were mighty confused. Here they were... or maybe there they were...well, wherever the hell they were...other than in room 311? Other than at the point Way Off? Okay, so the 312ians, as one might expect, if one has expectations, whoever one might be...oh, damn. Let's try again. The 312ians were having class in room 312 (obviously) and then the 311ers just rushed in and started telling them, "All wrong!   All...wrong!" so needless to say, the 312ians were flummoxed—which means confused. But you probably know that. Just like I don't have to say anything that's "needless to say," so pretend I didn't say it. Particularly since that was a long way for a brief recap.

After the 311ers pointed out that the 312ians were doing it "All wrong," they, being the 311ers, picked up the replica of the Sunsphere and began to list off exactly what was erroneous, passing the model back and forth to each other, and then forth and back—which, if you've never seen it, is quite a sight. All the while a group of 311ers noted down the problems and began making purchase orders. Or, at least they demanded that the underling 312ians make purchase orders, who demanded that other lower rung 312ians make purchase orders and...well, [sigh] while the 311ers with the Sunsphere spoke people wrote-transcribed-scribbled and sent pieces of paper away; what happened to be on those pieces of paper is uncertain. What was certain: the 311er complaints were ample:

First was the tile: "This tile's no good." Next were the decorations, or lack thereof (or of their lack, depending on how you approach it): "The walls and the ceiling are bare. Where's the damned decorations?" Then the windows: "How come there aren't any windows in here?" The lights: "Fluorescent?! Just about the worst kinda lights you could get!" And the blackboard: "Oh, I don't know, the blackboard seems fine...wait a minute! It's not black! Who ever heard of a blackboard that's not black? Can't hardly be a blackboard without being black, now can it?"

Which was true. In 312, the blackboard was green, as green as a...well, you know. Green? Of course the blackboard in 311 was probably green also, since the rooms were pretty much almost just about precisely similar, but...

When the lists were made and the orders put out, or at least when the writers stopped writing and sent their pages into the world, the 311ers ditched the Sunsphere by throwing it aside, where it rolled into a corner. Ditched because, if they could, the 311ers would have heaved it (being the replica) into a ditch, but no ditches being present, they had to compromise and accept the metaphorical colloquialism. At first they were not willing to accept this, and there was some discussion of building a ditch. There were even committees formed and laborers hired to survey the room to find the best location for a ditch. But in the end the 311ers said: "We accept the metaphorical colloquialism." Although, on second thought, I don't recall them saying anything of the sort. And the committees and laborers continued with their work, while others commenced bashing through the greenboard with a paperweight.

Ditches and metaphors, though, weren't on the mind of a particular 312ian who was sitting in the corner; she or he or whoever picked up the replica of the Sunsphere and rose, posing next to the model of World's Fair Park, as if to say, "My fellow personages, 311ers and 312ians alike. Why are we doing this to ourselves? Why are we bashing through our greenboard with a paperweight? It is a beautiful greenboard, leave it as it is. Much as we are beautiful people, 311ers and 312ians together. Why do we focus on such petty distinctions? We should unite. We should be as one." Or, at least, that's what it looked like he or possibly she was going to say. We'll never know. Because the leader, or whoever that person was who said, "All wrong," had him silenced—him being the 312ian who almost spoke the aforementioned speech, although said person's gender is certainly unknown, but then one can hardly call a person it, since it is the way things are supposed to be done in classrooms, and the 312ian was most assuredly part of that, or the wrong way. The point Way Off.

Clear as the summer's sun, no?

Yet, truth be told, the preceding argument is moot, for the revolutionary was silenced, turned mum, and anyone turned mum soon finds their mouth filled with wax, their skin the color of tar or asphalt or some other bituminous substance, their body wrapped in bandages; yes, a person turned mum is a mummy, an ancient Egyptian walking around the room, groaning and growling incoherently filled with the rage of knowing there is something to say, but not being able to say it. At least, that's the theory. Since mummies can't talk, no one actually knows. And since no one saw the revolutionary's skin transform or witnessed her or perhaps his mouth fill with wax... And since no one heard the revolutionary speak a single word, it just looked like s/he was going to talk... Hell, really, all anyone knows is that suddenly there was a being who rather closely resembled a mummy in the room, who happened to be holding the Sunsphere, until that being dropped the replica and began shuffling about, destroying everything in his/her way.

Around this time (whatever time that may be, since there were no clocks), the 311ers completed the demolition of the greenboard; the evidence: a pile of slate shards or whatever greenboards happen to be made of left on the ground. But the 312ians were no longer interested in the greenboard (a good thing, since it no longer existed (although it, the way things are supposed to be done in classrooms still existed, only the it that was the greenboard no longer did)); instead, the 312ians were now interested in the ancient Egyptian covered in bandages—the mummy. They were interested in the mummy, not in a going to the art museum as a child, seeing a great many boring exhibits, parents not letting you sit down, saying you're young, you should be able to walk twice, no three times as far as the adults, and, no, you can't have an ice cream cone, all you eat is junk food, we're here to get some culture, don't you want some culture, or do you want to grow up ignorant, a slack-jawed yokel like your Uncle Frank, and just when you thought you couldn't take it any longer, there, there in front of you was the Egyptian exhibit, the pyramids, the masks, the bizarre stories and beliefs, and, ah, yes, even the mummies, the mummies, the mummies, you were most interested in the mummies, and then, later, after grade school, after high school, in college, getting good grades in your classes, but still unsure of a major, all the majors seeming equally lame, really you're only getting good grades so that way you won't have to drop out and get a job, so the parents will keep footing the bills, and since school is so easy for you anyhow, getting good grades can be done with a hangover, can really be accomplished whilst high, out-and-out stoned, life one big party, one big avoidance of the future, until..., until you sign up for Archeology 101 and find that your fascination with mummies was not just a flight of childhood fancy, it was an honest to goodness interest, so you change your major from Undecided to Anthropology, ace the GRE, get into the University of Chicago, earn your Ph.D. in Anthropology/Egyptology, travel to Egypt and write the definitive book on the mummy sort of way, no, that wasn't the 312ian interest at all. Not for each and every 312ian, anyhow. Perhaps there was one... Anyway, the 312ian interest was in the fact that one of their own was transformed into a mummy. And things like that certainly didn't happen in the old days, back before the 311ers came roaring in with all their hot air and their big ideas. One of the 311ers even picked up the Sunsphere off a desk and kicked it across the room.

A particularly angry 312ian was going to complain, was going to say (you could tell by the look in his or her eye), "Hey, you can't turn one of ours into a mummy and bash our greenboard down and kick our replica of the Sunsphere across the room and expect us to sit idly by!" and it looked as if, after s/he made this speech, that s/he was going to wrathfully shake a fist in the air. You could just tell. Maybe you had to be there, but you could just tell.

But whatever the new complainer was going to say, well it doesn't matter because he or she was also immediately turned into a mummy, who instantly began groaning and growling and trashing the room. Now there were two mummies (which meant the number of mummy attacks and mummy related injuries skyrocketed), so the rest of the 312ians, being a timid bunch in the first place, kept quiet, zipped up their lips, all with stainless steel zippers.

Now the 311ers, as they found more and more wrong with 312, became piping mad because, as in times of old, those who were angry were known for playing the pipes, either bagpipes or waterpipes, and what happened was the enraged folks would bang and bang on the waterpipes, sometimes accompanied by furious friends on the bagpipes, and they would continue with this piping routine, pumping out a really incensed version of "Amazing Grace" (or that's what I figure since I can't think of any other song to play on the bagpipes), until all of their aggression was out and they fell over, either short of breath or with tired arms, and they'd drink a drink for the irate pipers who could no longer be with them because they had passed away due to heart attacks and ruptured arteries, and...

Where was I?

Oh, yeah.

The 311ers were so incensed they were putting off heat, their body temperatures still high from being in the overly warm 312, which in and of itself was making 311 warmer. Hence, because of convection, the temperature between the two rooms was now reaching a uniform degree. But the 311ers were still steaming, perhaps because of all the work on the ditch and the greenboard and the speeches and the purchase orders and, of course, they too were avoiding the semi-sentient, although highly destructive mummies, who were really making a mess of the place.

To expel their heat, the 311ers continued with their changes—and next up were the desks.

"Look at these desks! How could you have a class with desks like these? We're going to have to order new ones," said the "All wrong" guy, who felt so important he then added, "All wrong," and once more for dramatic emphasis, "All...wrong." But now, in hindsight, it might have been a different guy than the original "All wrong" guy, I'm not really sure, and any one of them could've been a gal, regardless, not to mention that the 311ers and the 312ians were starting to look similar because some 312ians, infected by 311er heat, had joined the 311er cause, and vice versa and verse vice-ah, so everything was getting pretty confusing.

Since the old desks had to go, the 311ers (although preempted, in some cases, by the mummies) started to bust them up. You might wonder, if you're the wondering sort, and you just may be, but if you're not pretend that you are and that you've wondered why the 311ers decided to bust up the desks when the desks in 311 were exactly the same. Well, it's all because the only way to bust anything is to bust it in an upwards direction. Nothing has ever been busted downwards, it's just not heard of. Once a man, or perhaps a woman, claimed to have busted something downwards, and there was a big tumult over the entire deal, and from the beginning the skeptics were skeptical, and the believers believed, the experimenters called for experiments, and the bystanders stood by, but in the end it was all a bunch of hooey—or perhaps only a moderate amount of hooey, depending on how much hooey you're used to and whether you're using the English or the metric scale of hooey measuring.

The 312ians, then, got out of their desks and the 311ers began to thrash the hell out of them (them being the desks) in the hopes of saving the souls imbedded in the hells imbedded in the desks because, I suppose, they were sent there unjustly by a desk god, and if the 311ers didn't save them, they would burn for eternity in that piece of schoolroom furniture. Now, if you are the inquisitive type, the type who makes inquisitions, then you probably think this was good work that the 311ers were doing; if you are not the inquisitive type, you perhaps are questioning why there are hells in desks, which merely shows that you are the inquisitive type (since you are asking a question) and therefore you lied when you said you were not the inquisitive type, or, alas, you do not know the definition of the word "inquisitive," or that you are shy about being the inquisitive type, and although the type fits you to a T, you coyly pretend that, no, not me, I'm not the kind of person who asks questions, but just this once,

I was wondering why there are hells in desks. It doesn't seem to make any sense. You just can't imagine it. But then, imagine this:

You're sitting in a classroom, the door opens, all of the people from the adjacent room come pouring in and the place starts to heat up fast because through the doorway there's this big, noisy floor fan blowing all the hot air from over there, over here and they start telling you "All wrong," and "All...wrong," and they bash down your greenboard and they turn some of your own into mummies (who wreak the expected havoc) and you're so afraid to talk you zip up your lips with stainless steel zippers and they make plans to dig ditches just so they can ditch a little replica and they decide everything needs to be replaced and then some of your own join them and some of their own join you and nobody can tell who's on whose side and then they take to busting up your desks. Can you imagine that? Can you? I sure as hell can't.

Finally, a couple 312ians (or whoever they were) couldn't take it anymore (it being the desk destruction (not the greenboard (and certainly not the way things should be done in classrooms))), so they unzipped their mouths and were about to ask, in unison, "Dear sirs [and madams], what in blazes is occurring here? We have examined the entire scenario, and we have no qualms with informing you that we are utterly and totally incapable of supplying an elucidating exegesis. Hence, we demand that you cease and desist posthaste." They also had the look of a couple that would shake their fingers in the air as they spoke.

Of course neither of them got a chance to speak because they were silencioed, as someone speaking Spanish for a brief period of time might say, if one happened to be walking by, which there wasn't, but just pretend; and that's why two more of the 312ians were turned into mummies...not because a hypothetical partially-Spanish-speaking person might have been walking by, but, well, you get the idea...

Thrashing the desks made the 311ers even hotter under their collective collars (perhaps on account of all of the hells they were liberating), but now they seemed to enjoy the heat, to revel in it, so they continued with their destruction by demolishing the tile and trying to hack some windows into the walls and shredding the model of World's Fair Park (which certainly didn't belong in a classroom) and generally outdoing the mummies' destruction, which had been random and sometimes avoidable, by breaking anything and everything, or even everything and anything into pieces; then, the pieces were hung from the ceiling, and the pieces hanging from the ceiling looked like burnt out stars in the sky. Luckily, the 311ers did not destroy the lights, otherwise it would have been black as pitch, which is even blacker than...well, it's really black. Take my word for it.

During the hubbub, someone tried to hang the little Sunsphere from the ceiling, possibly in an attempt to

instill order in the room, to make it appear as if the
entire farrago (although it was more of a foul-a-go)
was, in a way, structured around an esoteric design
which hid the answer to any inquiry one might happen upon; indeed, if one would merely look at the
supposed insanity, and employ a modicum of wit, one
would certainly come to a universal understanding that
had almost literally been staring one right in the face,
and it would be nigh maddening to see how simple,
how confoundedly elementary it had all been this entire time; but once the small model was in place, it fell
down again, bouncing on its golden dome and rolling
into the corner.

The 311ers were cooling down, so they began planning. They'd already ordered new desks, tile, and lights;
there were windows on the way, also (but where they
were going to go, no one knew). Then one of the
311ers asked:

"Like who you guys reading, anyway?" using the
word guys in a collective fashion, since he or she was
addressing both guys and gals...and mummies for that
matter, who had ceased their own destruction when
outdone by the 311ers.

Of course none of the zippered 312ians spoke.

"You reading...?"

They weren't.

"How about...?"

No again.

"Well, you have to be reading..."

No dice on that one either, but if there had been any dice, one might hypothesize if one is in the habit of hypothesizing that the roll would have come up snake-eyes, since the 312ians had not been reading that particular writer or book.

"What the hell you reading then?"

One of the mummies growled incoherently, which turned out to be a good enough reason for the 311ers to reestablish the destructive mood by tearing through all of the books in the room, then subsequently ordering new ones.

All the while the 311ers gave off more and more heat and seemed less and less energetic. Before they were galvanized, full of power, ripping things to shreds, making changes, planning ditches, turning people into mummies. Now they were brooding on the floor amongst the detritus. What were they doing in room 312, anyway? They were 311ers. It had appeared to be such a marvelous idea, back then. Before. There was fervor. There was enthusiasm. There were ideals, plans, expectations. There was energy. Now what was there? One of the 311ers picked up the Sunsphere, possibly hoping to rekindle the spirit of old, but then just dropped it.

When the desks, lights, tile, windows, and trenching equipment arrived, no one cared. But then the leader... oh, hell with it...some 311er hoisted the Sunsphere into the air and catalyzed the troops. In no time the new desks, lights, and tile were destroyed by the trenching equipped 311ers. Then the books showed up, and they were destroyed. The mummies punched holes in the walls and tried to strangle people, but luckily they were stopped; so they went back to groaning and growling. Soon the 311ers were just milling about the room, groaning and growling themselves. People began putting desks back together. Laying tile. Since most of the books were torn, they were fused together with the old books. The new lights were fluorescent. The tile was the same as before. The desks were similar, too. Everything took on a new aura, though, on account of being amalgamated.

There were still the burnt out stars hanging from the ceiling, though. But there was no order. The Sunsphere was lying on the floor, where it landed after its fall.

But even though everything was the same, it was subtly different in that way things can be different when they're no longer exactly the same, not exactly one hundred percent like they were before. Room 312 being similar, but not the same, made 311ers and 312ians alike nostalgic for the 312 of yesteryear, before the model of World's Fair Park was demolished, before the advent of the mummies (who no one knew how to turn back into regular people).

Cooled now, the 311ers saw no reason to remain in 312. And the 312ians never wanted the 311ers around in the first place. So most of the 311ers started to go back, along with the turncoat 312ians, and minus the equally turncoat 311ers. There was some question as to whether the door between 311 and 312 should stay open; or whether it should be closed but remain unlocked; or whether it should be closed and locked but that a vent should be installed so the two sides could converse. There were arguments for each stance. And there were adamant folks who wanted to know what to do with the mummies. In the end, the door was closed and was to be kept closed forever and ever using the door-propping-open technique that led to all the problems in the first place; no one knew what to do with the mummies, so nothing was done.

After the last 311er (or possibly a turncoat 312ian) departed, and the door was sealed shut, the heat level began to rise in room 312, which made the mummies more irritable so they began to attack more fervently, throwing on strangleholds and the like, and the collected inhabitants of 312 started to get pretty miffed themselves, and one of the former 311ers who stayed behind, or maybe he or she was an unmummified revolutionary 312ian, in the face of how miserable everything was, looked over at the door leading to 313 and decided that over there, in that room next door, yeah, the one Right. Next. Door, well over there they're doing it ALL WRONG! And to prove his, or possibly her point, right as he or she was about to demand that someone kick down that door to 313, the speaker put a foot down, which made a loud crunch: for underneath the foot was the five inch replica of the Sunsphere.

JACLYN DWYER
BIOGRAPHY OF A PORN STAR:
IN THREE PARTS

EXHIBIT A:

Solanacaea and Sores

At home, Michelle. Little Michelle. Blonde darling in a full house of blonde darlings. Mormons are always blonde, full and fresh. Nubile darlings. But she held the charm, gap-toothed smile told it all. Atropa belladonna, Deadly Nightshade, planted once, returns every year. A hallucinogen, swallow and swap sight for visions. Toxic atropine, ocular-dilator, the pupils of the eyes swell. Large onyx coins stare into the open lens, smiling. Always smiling. Always open, until the rogue taxidermist enters the frame.

: Turn over. Like this? Turn over. You want it in where?

A wincing smile escaped between her thick butterfly lips. Gap-teeth showing between her cheeks, smushed between a stranger's palm and the floor. Her very first time on screen. Head twisted so far, the bones bordered upon internal decapitation. YES YESYES YES After her first, she cried, returned to Utah, her Mormon mother's arms. Open. Waiting. When she confessed she more than modeled negligees, as she'd promised Mother. More than one man fucking (no missionaries, no mating as God intended) as they had promised her.

On screen, our Bella is a dark Italian beauty. A sacrifice for the stage it is so difficult to give up a towhead. So easy to cover the roots. Brunette bella, a pin cushion lover who speaks in acronyms DP. ATM. A toy, cubed. Blue latex missile3 + (stretched anal orifice) = XXX. A baseball bat. Louisville Slugger inserted fat end first into her ass. Five men. Six. Ten. Twelve. Our dark beauty performs. Loves performing. Smiles while she works, gaping gap-toothed smile, and it is work.

: Stop. I mean go. Never say no.

Was it because we raised her in the church? We didn't expect her to be a lawyer. We also didn't expect this. Even after she becomes sick, cured with doxycycline, azithromycin, becomes sick again. Incurable rash that isn't a rash. Red spots surface, spread over her ass in a constellation of sores. She is not the only one. She is the only one who retires. Every other year she retires, runs home. Hides. Sequestered. Quarantined, until she fills her prescription.

Every other year, our beauty returns to the hills, the unforgettable hills to shoot and film and smile while strangers, en masse, take turns masturbating onto her face. The gap in her teeth catches the white film, squeezes it out. Bella baby spits and swallows spits and swallows, teasing the cum into a frothy foam not unlike the root beer she was forbidden to drink back home.

: Never, ever say no.

EXHIBIT B:

A. belladonna

Signature smile reveals her exquisite allure. Scintillating incisors, iridescent onscreen, the print of Sainte Venus' seal. *Gat-tothed I was, and that bicam me weel*, a prelude to the wife our Bella would become. Belladonna. A girl known by only one name. Britney. Paris. Madonna.

Atropine extracted from our Deadly Nightshade is the antidote to mustard gas, makes the heart race, soothes the bleeding belly of fertile women. (That time of month, they don't perform, not even our blushing Bella with her blossomingly busy bottom). BREAK.

Bella's body is bent, Olympic dreams twisted into a contorted celebutante as her limbs become the arced wings of a soft pretzel. Our American darling competes with Chinese gymnasts, prepubescent girls revealing their pubises on primetime NBC. Soft line of the illiac crest smoothes into the indiscernible ischium. Twin bones joined together at the pubic symphysis. The pelvic girdle holds the belly in. Uterus Bladder Anus-intestine. Bella pees onto the floor. Sasha pees into

Bella's stretched sphincter. Bella laps at the liquid spill-age, a quadruped in pigtails.

Bella does anal. Bella does creampie. Bella does anal creampie.

Famous Polyphemus, one-eyed monster lurks in an undiscovered cave. Our Bella returns from retirement to sport an eye patch. She still loves to suck. Bella gags, is gagged again and again. Soft palate contractions stimulated by the glossopharyngeal nerve. *Gimme that good spit baby. Let it out. Don't let up.* Bella chokes while choking his chicken. His and His and His. Mucous and bile emitted from her empty belly. A natural lube. Bella must fast before each scene. Fast days before each film to clean herself out until she empty. Hollow inside. Clear water pours from her enema. Proof.

Bella deepthroats. Bella does double anal. Bella fucks with a pink pacifier in her mouth.

Bella smiles even as she's sucking a stranger's bent cock. Bella lets him blind her with salt as he misses her mouth, eyes squeezed shut, as a child diving into a cold pool. Crows stamp their feet at the corners of her eyes, but no, she's not crying, our Bella still smil-ing, satisfied with her success as she's made this man come. And that one and him, and her, and the next. Bella blinks, wipes her eyes, licks her face, but no it's not tears that she's tasting, a saline smear.

EXHIBIT C:

Twilight

Witches mixed our magic belladonna, Atropa B. with opium, hemlock, to procure a flying ointment. With this, they would aloft into the amorphous eve, straddling broomsticks, steering with their gnarled hands. Bubble Bubble Toil and Queen Victoria swallowed belladonna to numb the pain and blunt the practice of bearing a king, her own usurper, a successor to her bloody thrown.

Shadows waltz across our starlet's moon-faced cheeks, fishhooked by three fingers in her face, stretching her skin to expose her treated teeth. The demented dentist leads the bride in shearling boots and white sweats around an empty room. Her arms pinned behind her back, bound by twine that is not there. Elbows kiss each other. Wrists overlap. *Hold the pose.* This is not bondage because she is not bound.

Diane Sawyer investigates Belladonna's signature smile: *I want people to like me. I want people to think that I'm happy.*

Our porn queen (quean?), the stoic, cries only behind closed doors and only for undisclosed reasons. It is not her fault that women interrogate and berate other women until they cry. It is not her fault that her words have been cut and pasted and scrapbooked and saved then repeated, blunt sounds, against her own will. Bella flees this sad city where people throw stones – LET HE AMONG YOU WHO HAS NOT... CAST

THE FIRST LOT.

The witches' flying ointment was also used to induce twilight sleep, an anesthesia administered during abortions, where the patient is only half awake but fully aware. (the fetus is not a patient, but it is fully awake and possibly aware, if fetuses are indeed capable of the consciousness that carries awareness). But our Bella never miscarries, delivers her daughter, Myla, a diminutive of mine.

No. no. That's not what I said. See the smile? See how far I've flown? If I didn't want to, I wouldn't have leapt at all.

Our Bella soars, colorful wings of an Asian dragon tattooed over her left breast. They beat against her heart, flap when she bounces on top, when she feature dances, braiding her limbs around a brass pole. When she returns home, Bella unlocks her PO Box, reads her fanmail. Even this is on film, Bella has made it. Bella, our (porn) star. And Lot's wife doesn't even get a name.

The World

The army field manual defines torture. They are incapable of speech, being bound eyes and fingers wide. the army field manual defines a knife. your brain is almost entirely correlated, its fish-scents withstanding blue wrinkling, to a pot of boiling water. You wear these sequins like semi-precious gemstones. Oh lover lover me before this love is over. Rattle your teeth in a crock-pot monologue sky-side. a liquid reminder of the ubiquity of email. eye and finger-wide welts.

The rain falls continually on my tiny boat. The sound of television static or the sound of a microwave on high for three and a half hours. Your wildberry frosted poptart has finished cooking. We recline on a displaced bench seat from an oldsmobile. Gargle salt like lime ticks, say this is the way our president feels. t.s. eliot our emotions, immediately, with clarinet force.

ahh ohh ooo aaah uhhh thth ith the way the thungh feelth outh of my mouth. This is the way bleach works and the way it works and works. A full archive of public works projects on high. A mellifluous monologue about wireless connectivity and muscle striation. Contracted and exfoliated means of obtaining calm. Mellifluous is perfect there, muscles only grow. A penis-flex. We are fetishizing our bones, each one, the cartilage too. I am in love with the way your spine wears its scoliosis.

In the meat packing plant of unrestricted desire sing high—a man does not a bovine equal/a slop shop paintjob.

Our asbestos is reaping the benefits of our passionate cultivation. Cancer now is a cultural myth, a massive unequalizer, a sign of wealth. The swollen hands in the night watch should not be mimicked by the aspiring painters. The furniture slowly grows into other furniture. An infestation of June bugs in our esophagus. a royal rumbling of antiquity in the guest room we say, pick 'em, look look, them there, those 'uns.

A pianist on crystal meth, on high. This is the ambivalence we grew into. Flea market of the mental life, clothes hamper of the mental life. The metropolis and the garbage can a sentence raised to the hundreth power magnetized repeat five thousand times. Manifesto. NASA engineered aquatic landing. Nassau beach hotel. A womb-less whale, a collectible carving. Bone-heavy. Crow-blue. A crow's neck. Duck-snout. Raised to the tenth power. Raised to the hundredth power. Repeat. Manifesto.

The Words

   All of my lexicons are flimsy in this waterlogged washroom. They grow temporal boundaries like holy texts at high noon. I listen to the cowboy wailing for his mother among cowboys. The first dirty joke I learned was about a pair of tits in a tub. I stared at my hairless second-grade penis in the shower for hours.

   Ours is a bible without words, only sentence diagrams. Ours is a sentence diagram masquerading as a hangman. A polaroid of the remains swinging low in the Spanish moss.

   We forget what buttons we pushed, we pushed others. Measure my potency in ounces, use the shorthand. We calibrate our watches so that we don't need history books. Email me a list of ahistorical anecdotes. A veritable whale. Frosty midget-sized poems about rain on a tiny boat. The sound of television static. The sound of a microwave on high for seventy five seconds. Your thanksgiving dinner has finished cooking. The victuals were never enough. We are incarcerated in this incinerator. The generator is powered by bones macerated and intravenously injected.

   Manifesto. Repeated five thousand times. a phantasm of hand. Clown-blue eyes and a fragment of skull. Don't worry about cosmic interface. Grey-blue crater eyes and a Boniface skull. don't worry about golden sunsets. North Americans are plotting eastwards. Manifestos are repeated five thousand times on the evening news. heart attacks and colonoscopies are standard fare at the hospital of your choice. Doctors are receptacles for endless cash-advances. Nurses are feeding test-tube babies in the endless warehouse. Sunset bleak round country at the edge of the ocean. Bleak round clown skull at the edge of cosmic sunsets. Crow eat crow weather and the documents of faith based initiative. German people who sell whoppers who don't speak English. give me your sick and cover me with your HMO plans. Cover me with automatic weapon fire. wait your fucking turn and the animal zoo of disambiguation will Softsoap your concerns.

I read too many history books written by Neo-Nazis. The symbols grow into other symbols. Grow into hieroglyphics etched into the roughshod walls of our schoolhouses. This is not the way a good boy wears his welts.

This Man

Swing low—a man does not a tractor equal, the June bugs embedded. The hands, bone-stiff. Probing proboscis-like, south side. This is not the wheat we were meant to reap I am finding body parts scattered across my lawn. I am having a coronation party for my plot. I am dizzy with the white sinks in the red windows.

I am not the god you wanted but you already clicked send without double checking the address and these mistakes happen. I need more catchy one-liners in my daily speech patterns. I need clichés to be the rage again and for your tongue to be less in league with your lovely milk bone teeth. I need an honorary title because I am nothing but contents and footnotes and I am feeling like acid reflux runs my life. We are the aftermarket parts you forgot to put on your car. we are too fast on the collection of dead skin and moth wings and too furious a parade to be dismembered by so few swords. I am on a weapons kick. Love me for my serration my endless gunmetal surface.

Love me for the various oncology texts I have pro-duced. Love me for the way I found you wanting in the most flannel winter. I am a collection of microforms detailing the happenings of the most insignificant battle in the history of the world.

Hello ragged fourth grade caricature. Hello subset in a narrow room. Hello. Hello. Hello. I know. I know where it's taking me. I know the signs. Prognoses. Symptom-ology lollards mummers weaklings panic. Wooden pillows. Those lip-hangs from under your arms, those heart passages that gargle their own salt fluid, those regenerating anuses of dug worms, displaced brains slipping between moments of clarity on the medical charts. The way they are all looking at you. They know. And you know. Say it. Say it. I can't believe that the milk teeth of infants grow into incisors that meet the meat of grain fed things. So intuitively.

I am operating on an electric hum, the white noise of my daydreams. Dumbing down the parameters for self-reflexivity. A bank teller surrounded by a moat of words. Cash is so liquefiable she says good morning like a fire rages in the vault. I say welcome to the paper-shredder of modern exceptionalism. She says would you like a receipt? I paw out my bones through the rocky course of my esophagus, sputter my marrow through the splinter sized holes in my teeth. I say sure. Surely something more. I clutch at straws, miss the value of my word bank. Would you like me to make you a new operating system? I will call it laundry chute.

RYAN CALL
SOMEWHERE AHEAD SMOKED
THE WRECKAGE OF MY
EVENING

That summer my parents hadn't yet journeyed into the saw-toothed arena of their divorce; instead they tiptoed around it for some time, lingering hazily in the vague countryside beyond, the divided landscape of their relationship. Such was their loveless cohabitation: had they but noticed me, their young son, they might have prevented my stumbling into a similarly underwhelming failure.

My then-girlfriend, a weak facsimile of a woman, liked her boyfriends weather-beaten and tired. I had driven for almost an hour through torrential rain to join her at some weekend pool party, a long way to go back then for a chance at dry-humping in a tool shed. If she felt courageous, we might heavy-pet each other, though I'd learned not to expect that awkward hobbyhorse at every meeting. We had been in high school for an unimportant amount of time, and I should not have been a virgin.

Thunderstorms converged above the neighborhood that night, making swimming and diving an electric activity from which we all unhappily excused ourselves. Instead, we made it a long evening, drinking cough syrup from the medicine cabinet and rat-tailing the other sexes with our beach towels.

I strayed away from the group to get another bottle and found a drunken girl draped over the couch in the family room. The top of her head almost touched the floor. I could hear my girlfriend's voice in the basement. I had left her with a handful of darts, which she'd begun to toss lamely at things, laughing.

This house is so big, I told the girl.

You're drunk, she said into the fabric.

I am simply very thirsty, I said.

This house is enormous, I said.

I'm not, she said. Drunk, she said.

Gigantic, I said.

You'd think so, she said.

I know so, I said.

You want to take a look around, she said.

I know so, I said.

Despite my loudly interacting with everyone in the basement, I felt that I had passed into a ghostly state of social irrelevance. I uselessly repeated words and phrases, enunciated carefully those brief communications that had functioned so well for me earlier in the evening. When I spoke, my language exploded away from my face like a burst tire, its fragments cartwheeling across the highway.

On the second floor we found the master bath-room and shower, a gaudy affair with multiple nozzles, a slotted bench, clear glass all around, more soap dishes than necessary. It made sense that we should turn on the water, what with so many pipes in want of use, and soon we had undressed. I'd never noticed her before: the slight promise of her breasts, how her stomach pouted just above the patch of her hair, the way her thighs sadly touched below the mysterious point of her crotch. The simplicity of her nakedness, the hoary sheen of it, alarmed me, and before I could cup myself, hide myself in my hands, she guided me into the shower stall and tugged at the water dial.

We stood together beneath the scalding jets of water that crashed into our skin, making us tremble like plants. Steam fogged the entire world of the bath-room, and the girl leaned against me, water pooling in the hollows of her collarbone. She blinked her eyes beneath the points of her bangs. I allowed her to turn me around, and she kneaded my body with her slender hands. She began to wash me.

* * *

I ceased relations with my girlfriend the next day after a pensive phone conversation about God and my sacred life. Back then, my girlfriend and I spoke in a backdoor-y sort of manner; we had discovered how certain words offered a way out of a conversa-tion when another person tried to get in, and for that reason I hung up on her. I didn't expect her to follow up on the discussion, to emphasize her status as the person whom I'd wronged.

But, after lunch, she came over to the house. She wore bandages on her hands and fingers to hide the stigmata of her darts-play, and in her backpack she carried a number of photo albums documenting our relationship, all of the different places in which we had fumbled together. I suppose she planned to examine these with me, perhaps to stir up my passions, to make me realize what gentle experiences I'd forsaken, but my eyes were already strained on account of the sun shining through our skylights.

From the breakfast nook, my parents welcomed her and then returned to the inky grids of their newspapers. Because hers was a somewhat familiar face, one that demanded of them very little in the way of an emotional response, they often asked me if she'd like some small trinket to show their appreciation.

Perhaps a nice pair of earrings, my mother once had said.

Or earplugs, my father said and poured his coffee all over the kitchen floor.

I'd prepared a list of reasons why God should leave me alone, the first being that I'd grown tired of the my body/His temple school of thought. My girlfriend, for she hadn't yet recognized the legitimacy of the severance, thought this a rather laughable, but crude sort of complaint, and thus began our second breakup discussion of the day.

She had a solution, probably one she'd arrived at during the earlier days of our relationship. Hers was a semantic argument: the phrase heavy-petting had an innocent, charming feel about it, a softer meaning, which she found so lacking in the sad profanity of the terms mutual masturbation, vaginal intercourse, and the like.

You can guess, then, which activities were off-limits.

I pulled down the blinds of my window and suggested she do a bit more research into the sex-related jargon of our generation.

I don't know what you're talking about, she said.

Word combinations, I told her, such as blue-balls, might give you another perspective on the entire issue.

She shrugged at me, and I shrugged back to imitate her. She rolled over and lay facedown on my bed. I sat down next to her and stared at her head, the tangle of greasy hair at the base of her neck. I wanted to lick her somewhere.

My parents entered the room bearing celebratory gifts. They passed around chocolates and an instant camera. My girlfriend sat up abruptly and scooted away from me. I shielded my eyes from the flash.

You needn't feel embarrassed, they told her, mistaking her reddened cheeks for something entirely different than what I'd mistaken them for.

Your son, my now ex-girlfriend told them as she stood to go, has just broken off the relationship because I'm not carnal enough for him.

That's not what I said, I said.

I never said that, I said.

But she'd already distanced herself from the mean angles of our house, leaving me the task of throwing away the snotty balls of tissue paper that she had piled upon my nightstand.

* * *

The next few days found me pursuing an unlikely courtship with that girl from the shower. We embarked upon an official first date: a self-guided tour of the local train museum where we allowed some cheap machine to smash our pennies into small ovals of copper, the impressions on which we could not recognize. After school let out each day, we often walked the paths along the river, remarking the occasional dead fish floating in an iridescent slick of oil and a long, thin eight-oar-shell cutting through the deeper water. One weekend we dared each other to throw small rocks off the overpass, but then we could not find any rocks to our liking, so she took me to a pawnshop, where I purchased a warped violin for her, though we knew nothing about stringed instruments.

In the car, she rested the violin case on her lap and looked out of the window. I drove through the city and told her about my intense fear of running over pedestrians.

You're afraid, she said, is what you're telling me. You're generally a fearful person, she said.

I have this recurring daydream, I said. In it I'm driving up to an intersection and someone steps out from between two parked cars.

And whump, I said, he's gone beneath the front end.

So just be careful, she said. I have those dreams, and I am a careful person now.

Sometimes it's a person and a stroller, other times a child with a bicycle, I said.

That makes me feel a little less comfortable around you, she said.

Listen to me, please, I said, because this is important.

* * *

After a week or two of subtly inquiring into my status as a high school student in the midst of a fresh relationship, my parents invited my new girlfriend over for dinner without asking my permission.

We're your parents, they said. We don't need your permission.

I had wanted to ease my new girlfriend into a soft, feathery sense of my home: the subdued conflict of its leaders, the neat loneliness of the second floor, what not to touch or taste in the dining room. Things that I felt would best alert her to the ebb and flow that characterized my experience of familial love. I had in mind a lengthy period of preparation followed by brief moments of contact. Family and new girlfriend in passing trains, family and new girlfriend awkwardly meeting at bumper cars, family and new girlfriend eyeing each other from a distance, in a park, perhaps, full of unleashed dogs. I felt these situations might best provide a comfortable introduction to my parents so as to prevent her from separating herself from me for good.

At dinner, my parents competed for her attentions, for any sort of compliment she might send their way. My groaning father flexed his biceps above the kitchen table, and my mother cheerfully insulted the veins in his forehead.

Better than I can say about your legs, my father said.

What can you say about my legs, my mother said.

Two words, he said. Road maps, he said.

Three words, my mother said. Internet browser history, she said.

I looked up from grimacing into my noodles to see my new girlfriend wink at me. I understand, her wink suggested. Here you have something interesting going on and I'd like to go with it, her wink appeared to say. She seemed to appreciate their effort to tumble themselves into her lap, and after dessert she stacked the dishes around the sink, insisting that she couldn't possibly wash them, since they had just met.

* * *

We had recently overcome our awkwardness around

a manual transmission, and as we sat making out in the driveway of my house, she pulled away from me and wiped her nose. In the darkness of her car I couldn't tell if she had started crying or if she just needed to wipe her nose, but her next words made it an easy guess.

I love you, she said.

Oh, I said, not knowing what to do: a hard-on anchored me to the passenger seat, but my last relationship had taught me how badly I handled crying women.

My house sat atop a large, wooded hill, so I hoped that my obvious concern for our safety might give me a reasonable chance to formulate a response. I jiggled the shifter to make sure she hadn't knocked it out of gear.

Okay then, I said and opened the car door into the rain. See you later, I said.

Had I known then what a nuisance my evasion would cause for me, I might have chosen my words quite differently. But a boy living from one ejaculation to the next rarely concerns himself with those kinds of emotional scenarios.

I peeked out of the upstairs hall window. Her car still sat in the driveway, but the driver's side door hung open. A shadow stretched across the flagstones of our puddled front walk, and soon the doorbell buzzed loudly.

My parents, bathrobed and slippered, ushered her

into the house. They shouted my name and berated me from the comfort of the living room: how could I leave such a darling out in the wet weather? My mother's tea kettle whistled from the kitchen, and I realized that sleep no longer had a firm place in my near future. It looked as though my parents had made plans to blunder all of us through this supposed crisis until the early morning if need be.

They sat around our wrecked coffee table, palming steaming mugs to their pursed lips. I sensed a three-against-one by the curve of their shoulders, the thrust of their heads; there was a little bit of the huddle about them. My body sagged in protest. I took a clumsy seat in a wicker rocking chair and creaked my way towards a conversation opener.

I can explain everything, I said.

Son, my father said, you don't need to explain any-thing, we understand.

My father had managed to slick down one of his cowlicks, so he looked less ridiculous than my mother, whose robe had fallen away to reveal her legs, all prickly and varicosed. A small, gift-wrapped box sat on the table in front of my new girlfriend, though she seemed to have decided to ignore it for the time be-ing: a reasonable, self-interested decision in my opin-ion, but one my parents had not noticed. If this went badly for her, she could walk away without a junky keepsake.

We support your decision, my mother said, though

we find it a bit odd that you've not yet learned enough about this to know the consequences, given your complaints about your last girlfriend.

Love very much has to be a part of it, my father said.

My new girlfriend stared at me and I decided that she had privately retracted her earlier statements, both the one she had made to me in the car and whatever she had said to my parents upon entering the house. The sad way her smile had curled itself above her chin hinted as much. She looked uncomfortable, even ill.

We can't blame you, my mother said.

I suppose this is our fault too, my father said.

We never had the talk with you, my mother said.

The talk, I said.

Yes the talk, they said.

I got the talk in human development last year, I said.

The talk about sex, my father said, coughing.

The sex talk, my mother said.

Yes, I said. That talk. I've had it already.

Sex, they said, looking oddly at my new girlfriend.

No, I said, the talk.

I'm sorry, my father said.

We're a little confused now, my mother said.

I think we all are a little confused now, I said.

My new girlfriend quietly rose from the chair, shielded her face with her hands, and walked out of the house, leaving each of us to our own thoughts: my father clanked his spoon around in the lukewarm teacup and thought about pornography, when he might next have a chance to look at some on his computer; my mother went to the window to watch the car disappear down the driveway and thought about the word platonic, reminded herself to open a dictionary when she awoke the next morning; and I rocked stupidly in that chair and thought about how I might never lose it, how I would die alone in a commercial plane crash, having never once given myself away to those seated around me.

KRISTINA BORN
THE DEFINING WORK OF YOUR
CAREER
(EXCERPTS FROM *ONE HOUR OF
TELEVISION*)

110.

One day, an unexpected test will cause the people to break down. The test itself is not important; what matters is that the test is real and is coming. One day. And what will you do then. Wail in the street? Yes; for a time. But soon you will remember our face and be relieved. You will sit down with the other man, who has also stopped wailing, and wait. Neither of you will be run over because this is a rural road and is very rarely used.

33.

We resisted the creep of nuclear fuel for as long as we could, but when the big boys are colliding their naked selves in the proverbial arena, what are we as a nation to do but sit in the corner and oil them and hand them a towel? The point is, we are not the wrestling ones. If, for example, we'd been giving Muhammad Ali free fuel for his automobile, we wouldn't be hearing any complaints. In fact, none of this would even be seeing the light of day.

21.

Prior to the discovery of radiation, an arms race looked much different: we all stood back and let the other guy have a go. So now today when every little nation wants a turn we have to sit it down and explain exactly why it doesn't get one. We have to squat with our hands on our knees so that our face is level with its face and say, This is grown-up talk, sweetie. Mommy and Daddy are having a disagreement but they still love each other very much.

27.

The disagreement quickly escalated from a church problem to a world problem. We can tell because we've had extensive experience with both. You can tell because that country and that country are both on fire. If these countries were fireworks, we'd be standing back along the beach, daring each other to get our feet wet while we watched. Electrocution! we'd yell. But there'd be no electrocution. The girls would take their shirts off.

102.

A person was discovered in the debris of the first hydrogen bomb. When we asked him what he was doing there, he said, Where? Right here, we said. Oh. Here. Well, he said. We urged him to go on. I'm supposed to be here, he said. And we're not? we said. You said it, not me, he said. We stood astonished but started moving again after just a little while.

95.

"Money" is synthesized from money and has no known uses, except of course what we use it for. This could be any number of things, but we are aware that it is not inherently a part of reality. We wash our hands in anti-matter. We laugh at air running through our fingers.

39.

One thing we will do is massage the dead heart of Africa. It's not really dead! you say, and how can we reply? We agree. Take it to the doctor! you say, and we have to stop you there. These people don't believe in doctors, and that is something we must respect. They only believe in our two hands and what's in them when we hold them out. So right now what's in them is the dead heart of Africa, and we squeeze and release. Squeeze and squeeze and release.

30.

A nation's relationship with its bird has no known

biological role. You may love the bird very dearly but in the end you are eating a cow. What, then, is to prevent a nation from plastering a lizard on its face? A minotaur? Well, the people. The people have been told to finish what's on their plate.

12.

In any interactive portrait of a virtual village, there is always one child standing in the frame with her eyes rolled up into the back of her head. The other villagers are barefoot in the dirt; they have no idea. It's some glitch in the software. We draw a moustache on her face and then erase it. We shake the monitor and nothing falls out, not even a penny.

88.

Anesthesia machines can deliver a person from inhibition. They change how much a person is willing to confront in his life. For example, is he able to choke his whore of a wife to death while unconscious? No; not in any real way. There are stable and unstable forms of a person and the stable ones sleep. They tell us how glad they are whenever they open their eyes.

42.

There is a way to intentionally introduce impurities into something extremely pure. We do not know what it is just yet, but have been told, reliably, that it is very, very good. Of course the not knowing leads to myriad ethical questions, such as: when we learn it, does it become public knowledge? We are under no illusions that we are somehow the public but we are numerous and it needs to be said. And then, if it is indeed public knowledge, will a person off the street be capable of entering a library and learning what we know from a book? And if this is true, should we not then be systematically emptying our heads of all thought, so as to not just give the advantage over to the man in the street and basically forfeit the whole game?

131.

Say if we approached you in the street with these sorts of questions. It will be pouring rain and you will be trying to work your umbrella. We will stand in front of you, umbrella fully functioning, offering you no help with your umbrella. Possibly dressed all in black. Or something to indicate a sort of menace, but vaguely, you see. A gentle menace. Enough that you will notice but will not be able to put a finger on it and you will be irritated. Standing in front of you, we will ask loudly, over the rain, if a new opera could indeed be the defining work of your career. You will appear stunned. You will look up at us with a decided lack of recognition. "I don't work in opera," you will say. "I don't even like opera." And that will be the problem, will it not? You don't even like it.

CONOR MADIGAN
KLEMPT, LEVER PULLER

A woman waves hands above paper sheets on table before you and gazes over you knowingly, then paper sheets. You. Paper sheets. You. You don't know her. Recall this in your statement. Statement: I do not know her.

* * *

Klempt's grip crumples a twenty-dollar bill. "For me?" Klempt whispers. Decades of tenant handprints, splash-memories—slaughtered animals, greasy fingers smear walls of his dark room. A note: Linus: ten dollars. Linus lends money. A woman lives with Linus few see. She spits.

* * *

A naked man enters from under the table. Door below. He wears a horse's head blood spills steam from, and drips silver-hair chest. He blinks. A last blood spews and the man sees from horse eyes. You know him. He works levers with you at the factory. He slept with your sister and didn't bathe before. You hate him. The woman waves hands. Blood spatters paper sheets. Your stillness aches. Recall this in your statement. Statement: My stillness aches.

* * *

Klempt careens dark hallway to Linus's door. His eye flutters anticipation. Door opens and upon Klempt's face spit flings. He holds the bill forward. Linus pushes him back and slams a cockroach underfoot. Cockroaches flee. Bill departs Klempt's hand. Linus produces two bill-rolls, licks fervently the twenty-dollar bill, wraps it on one roll, peels off a five-dollar bill from the other, forces it in Klempt's small mouth, shouts, "My lunch!" Rubber-band snaps bill-roll behind closed door. Klempt murders many hallway roaches, some bigger than the rest. He considers he may have killed an oligarch, how splendid to win these small battles.

* * *

Horseheadman slaps his hands clumsily on table before you. Horse eyes consider paper sheets. Blood finds new ways from cavities inside horse's head. You consider the horse head must now be the man's for eyes view and mouth speaks, "You must choose." The woman kneels, sits and scoots into door below. You fear. Recall fear in your statement. Statement: I recall fear, for the unknown woman has left.

* * *

In his room Klempt towels off spittle. The five-dollar bill falls from his mouth. He examines pockmarks on his arms, liver spots. He flexes. He must address weakness. Pushups. He foots bed and hands floor to shoulder-press. Sweat beads where spittle dripped. He hates himself. Oxblood floor, he hates himself; single burner stove, he hates himself; dry-cleaned shirts from lost job six years back, he hates himself; passionless wife, he hates himself—no wife, he loathes himself; burnt hair from the whore, Aha, next door, he hates himself. Aha's face, blank, tired. Pain bites wrists. Klempt crawls to bathroom floor and massages arms.

* * *

You taste iron. Warm blood. The man's penis, balls, thighs and calves run it flowingly and fling blood to your face. He dances. Blood thickens air dank. Dances cease. The man sneezes inside and blood-bubbles neck, unsettles your one-legged-stool balance. You run exposed fear risk to ask why a man followed work at the levers factory with a dirty hand sister fuck. You gulp dry gulps. You dry heave. You croak some word like yourk, or yolk. You smile. Embarrassed. You force eye contact adoration. "I'm sorry?" horseman says. You cannot speak, so recall this in your statement. Statement: I am dumb.

* * *

On Klempt's mirror You're The Problem scrawled in lipstick dropped outside Aha's door. Klempt examines his face. His face resembles her child's, though he never visited whores. Klempt's approach for casual conversation hid the child behind Aha's leg. Child's face blanked when Klempt prefaced, "I'd like casual meals with you," with, "I know you're the whore, but." Klempt couldn't figure a child understanding the oldest trade.

* * *

Blood swells paper sheets. Seen, and heard, not felt or tasted, a woman, AGAIN. She waves a hand casually above paper sheets. She gazes at you knowingly. You know her as the woman from before. A bright corner floods the room. Sunlight requires emollient for chapped skin, you think. The woman ignores but knows it. She moves sound. Sound from her, louder than from—the horseman! sister-fucker left, you realize. Where did he go? "---!" you attempt. One legged stool fails and topples you. "You cannot speak," the woman says. You settle. "The horseman toyed with you. Didn't he?" You calm with her voice. Statement: I calm with her voice.

* * *

The lever factory scares Klempt. Aha scares Klempt. The lever factory broke many wrists and forearms, subsequent backs and legs. Aha knows only many. He fears this pain never felt. Wrists snapped. Lonely heart. How pain tastes metallic. How fear bubbles molten in his lungs. Aha.

* * *

Statement: Aha.

Kiddie Land

Cheryl lost her uterus when she was lucky number seven. She was riding a loopy roller coaster, sick on funnel cake, when the thing started to poke out at her underpants. "Cripes," was all Luci, her fifteen year old babysitter, could say when they examined the thing together in a restroom. Luci prodded at it with a cherry red fingernail detailed with a puffy paint unicorn head. The thing glopping between Cheryl's thighs was gooey and slick, like a newborn puppy.

"I think you're having babies, Cheryl. We should get a towel or something." Luci went to the dispenser and yanked several squares of rough paper towel from it, crumpling and packing them against her chest. "Here, use these," she said, holding a handful of them out for her charge, encouraging Cheryl to recline. They tucked a few of the towels under her tailbone, and the girls waited for something more to erupt from the little hole between Cheryl's legs. When nothing came but a few dribbles of thickish sap the color of melted mixed berry popsicle, they agreed to stuff her undies with a wad of scratchy towels and head out to the ferris wheel.

But not before Luci took her birth control. While the pills were really quite necessary, Luci took the things mostly because she enjoyed popping them through the thin aluminum backing of the pink pill cards. She liked the way the metal cracked, the sound of the pills rattling in their plastic pods, but most of all, she liked swallowing things. So, at noon every day, she took a few Thursdays, or a few Fridays—whatever the day, she ate three, keeping things consistent and very much in order.

It was a Tuesday, so Luci pitched three Tuesday triangles of birth control into her mouth and slurped a minute's worth of water from a gum-clogged drinking fountain. This is when it began. It was always strongest right after the pills. Luci's consumption of so much birth control caused her uterus to suck infants, even very small toddlers, into her prickly papoose, lined with thick layers of anti-baby. She walked by the teacups and, using only the supreme gravity of a uterus pumped with too many synthetic hormones, tore a six month-old boy from his umbrella stroller, snapping the plastic buckles around his waist, sucking him toward her poisonous chamber. The boy flew through the air and thudded against her pubic bone, squealing a bit as she slurped him inside. Near the red choo-choo, which circled the theme park, she robbed one car of a new-ish babe bundled like a soft parcel in its mother's arms and emptied another car of young twins, taking them all in like an industrial strength Hoover. This happened, and happened, and happened, until Cheryl began to complain again about the thing poking out between her legs. She said her inner thighs were beginning to chafe and asked if they could sit down somewhere or something.

The girls found an unoccupied bench near the merry-go-round. Luci slumped into it roughly, her chubby thighs bubbling out between the narrow strips of metal, her quickly-filling belly resting on her like a giant hive. Cheryl was a bit more delicate in her parking, as she could feel the thing waddling between her legs continue to nudge its way out, pulling on her insides. There was more of it now, she could tell, and her overalls were damp, probably with the same purplish sap they saw before. Then, all of a sudden, as Luci was taking in another child, the rip of baby backpack Velcro still pregnant in the air, Cheryl heard a sloppy sort of sound, she heaved kind of automatically, then quickly gave birth to the gummy slab that was her uterus.

It was very uncomfortable, squishing around in her pants, and very embarrassing that she had to ferret for it. Reaching down into her overalls with both hands,

Cheryl snatched a handful of something and squealed like she did the first time she touched the class hamster.

"God, Luci—what the heck?" she said, clenching her baby maker like it was a freshly caught trout.

"Oh...one of those. I wouldn't worry about it, anyway."

Ambrosia

Ambrosia Thumbington, 24, had a fashionable body; she was long, slim, her skin incredibly soft. She could be made of pipe cleaners. Hers was a body frequently noticed and highly regarded. Her milkman would have loved her body, too—those immeasurable smooth sticks, a tummy stretched taut as a drumhead, hipbones jutting from her abdomen like new mountains, elbows cut like fine gems—if he didn't drop by so early in the morning. The milkman noticed her azaleas, though, issuing their spring flesh, and that, it turned out, was enough.

It was the morning of a milk delivery when Ambrosia Thumbington, 24, died a horrible death at the hands, etc., of one serial rapist, Herman T. Plugg, who picked her up in his rusted out, piece of shit '87 Camaro featuring a dashboard hula girl whose coconuts, faded from daily abrasion, shook wildly as the car turned off the road and rolled substantially enough into a heavily wooded area adjacent to the highway. An empty hamburger wrapper floated around the back seat, another skirt teased up, but by the wind.

After he raped Ambrosia on the ground, he tied her to a tree with three scraps of frayed nylon twine and raped her again, the pine's sharp, plated bark and Herman's gnawing away at her flesh. Then he went to his car, came back and raped her with the same rusty tire iron he used to finish her off. The iron cracked her skull like a spoon into the toasted crown of fresh crème brûlée, its ramekin perfect and smooth.

But Ambrosia, quick in the wits, chose to return, as things do [return], as the cream-filled sponge cake known to children and adults alike as a Twinkie and was self-sufficient enough to maneuver her way into a particular box in the particular grocery store at which one Herman Plugg regularly did his grocery shopping, namely in the aisles of beer and snack cakes. While generally abstruse, it's possible for even supposedly inanimate objects to use their various preservative energies to attract particular things to them, in this case the driver [Herman Plugg] to Ambrosia, adding a sweetly ironic and indigestible twist to things.

It wasn't long before Herman Plugg's Camaro wrenched around a corner and into the grocery store's parking lot. The runny chords of some haphazard rock tune plipped out of a front speaker. Having picked up a bit of momentum for the turn, the driver aggressively and prematurely jammed his automobile into an available slot picked both for its convenience and availability. A bit crooked. He hit the brakes, jarring the hula girl. He reversed in order to straighten, jammed, braked, reversed, and jammed it in one final time, straight up the middle. Herman Plugg turned the car off, sauntered into the store, and made his way up the beer aisle. As he made his way down the snack aisle, more specifically to a particular box lined with ten golden, cream-filled cakes, alarmed when one of the cakes burst forth from the cardboard's perforated edge, shed its cellophane wrapping and thrust thoroughly into his trachea, a bit of oil leaked onto the hot pavement.

Rumors

The only thing we know for sure is that she has three breasts. There are rumors going around that she may have more than one vagina, but nobody so far has been willing to investigate.

We're afraid. We're afraid of the face we might make if there are two. Or, heaven help us, maybe more. In any case, we know the face we'd make would not impress. And besides, Mom always said if when you saw a woman with more than one vagina you made a face long enough, it might stay that way. And then, God, who knows what.

The Paragraphs

The Paragraphs lived a miscellaneous life, doing things in disconnected parts. They always got something started. Then, when things were getting going, they would stop and move on to something completely new.

One sundry Saturday the Paragraphs began packing. Into her portmanteau, mauve, Mrs. Paragraph stuffed a pair of generous sweatpants, two cotton tee shirts, a fitted charmeuse blouse, which emphasized her lovely shape, several pairs of underwear, some socks, her bright orange vanity bag filled with the appropriate things, and a small revolver with mother-of-pearl grip inlays gifted to her by an uncle who, at an early age, had shot off one of his big toes. Mrs. Paragraph picked the revolver up and held it against her face. Like a cold pillow, it soothed her.

Downstairs Mr. Paragraph was making level-five toast, browning his favorite white bread just so. While the bread was toasting, Mr. Paragraph located all of the possible spreads that he might use: strawberry jam, raspberry jam, butter, apple butter, peanut butter, honey. He set all of these spreads out on the counter, organizing them alphabetically, and leaned back against the kitchen's island, rubbing his chin thoughtfully. Mr. Paragraph noticed that, in this panorama of toppings, something was out of place. Was it the cat?

Mr. Paragraph forgot entirely about his toast while

Mrs. Paragraph unpacked her portmanteau. They stayed home that weekend, ate no toast, and thought about each other, but in different rooms.

Although the outer walls have been repainted, he easily recognizes the underlying structure as his own work. It is an odd structure, made up of more twists, obstructions, and complications than most of its kind, and seeing it again, though in a photograph, he again enjoys the labor of its construction, the fifteen years it took him to design and build, beginning when he was just out of college. He had not, at first, planned to build the structure, but only to see if he could make his thoughts correspond to the structure's edges, pressing against its walls, fitting to its corners, hovering at its windows as he transferred the structure to paper.

While he was drafting the structure, he discovered that by passing through one level in a particular series of movements—he had found only one series for which the end result would be true—he could pass through all of the structure's levels. Though he would have no sense of having moved upward or downward, and would feel as though he were only moving farther away from the place where he had started, what he called "the entry," nevertheless, he would have traversed all of the structure's levels, ending back at the entry. He had designed an impossible object. And in this discovery was another, more satisfying discovery: he knew that he could build it.

When it was finished, he gave it to his wife for a wedding present. He showed it to her only once before it was finished, when they had just begun dating, and though it was only a skeleton of the complete structure, he was excited to show it to someone, to have someone share its final shape's becoming, to touch its arching doorways and walls, and to make it real in the touching. She had been attentive, saying she knew how important the project had been to him for the many years when he had burrowed into working out its details nearly every night, after work, on weekends, filling boxes with drafts in which some flaw made the structure impossible to build, wanting to get everything right, every convexity, every concavity, every plane and every angle. She said she found the design original, having seen a few of a similar kind, but none so purposefully complicated as his and which caused her to experience the pleasure of surprise when, having thought she had been moving through many levels, further and further from the entry, she ended right back at the entry.

He felt relief finally to have another person say that she too experienced the strange feeling of ascending what was in fact a flat surface. They agreed they felt it most of all in their stomachs, and had compared it to the feeling of taking a turn in a car at a high speed, when the body wants to continue traveling forward but the walls of the car force the body to travel in a different direction.

He had given it to her when they married so that he could live in it and feel that his time inside it was a gift from her to him. They lived there together for nearly seven years.

She had asked for the divorce, and he had moved out.

At first, he missed the confusing yet satisfying puzzle of the gift's structure. But after a while of living on his own, he found that it was a relief to ascend real stairs to the door of his bachelor's apartment, where he had a drafting table for his work as an architect, and where he had a bed and a small refrigerator among few other possessions—though he made decent money, the desire to acquire objects eluded him like water does a convex surface. In his own apartment, he could think, I will go downstairs, and then really move his body down the stairs and out the door to the street, whereas when he had been living with his wife inside his gift to her, he or she would say, "It's downstairs," or, "I'm going upstairs," or, "Let's go upstairs," but only as a figure of speech, because they lacked words to describe what happened when they felt they were moving down or up one or several levels but knew that they were not, and where, it had seemed, they were speaking their own language simply by moving through what they came to call, for lack of a better word, their "house." In their house, when one of them said, "Let's go upstairs," the words seemed part of a game the house was playing with their bodies.

After living alone again for nearly as many years as he lived in the house, and having lost touch with his ex-wife, without searching, without wanting, really, to see the house again, he discovers, on a morning when he has read the newspaper through to the real estate section without awareness of what he's reading, that the house is for sale by someone named Gary.

Seeing a photograph of the house is enough to detach him from his routine and surroundings for some time. He sits in his apartment without being in his body, observing himself. Look at the man's posture. Look how he lets his jaw hang open while he doodles. Look how fat he's become. Look how his hair is matted and sticks up on one side—when was the last time he showered? He smells bad. Look, there are wrinkles around his eyes and lips now, and his upper arms are soft. God, smell him. His room is shabby. Covered with dust. He can afford to live better but doesn't see a point in the effort. He has become flat, dimensionless, with nothing except location, his musty apartment. Is he breathing? He masturbates in the shower. He must be alive then?

He sits at his drafting table with the ad he's clipped out of the paper, considering his entanglement with its meanings, making a little sketch of Gary—a fat belly connected to his ex-wife's face.

He knows that after the divorce his ex-wife lived in the house for a time. She would call occasionally to ask questions about the plumbing, the way he'd wired the switches, so that she would know what to tell the repair guy. But within a year she stopped calling, and she has not answered when he has tried, six times in total, to call her; the phone has gone on ringing. After the thirtieth or fortieth ring, the ring tone becomes not a sound but a series of pauses between affirmations that he is, in fact, alive. During those pauses weeks might go by, months, a year, his skin becoming flakier, his arms fleshier, his bathroom moldy, his dishes congealed, bruises he can't explain appearing on his body, then fading to greenish, then fading to flesh, then flaking off, accumulating in the corners, his bodily flesh renewing itself despite his inner disintegration.

Realizing he is distracted and accomplishing none of the work he's paid to do, he sets aside the sketch of Gary and dials the agent's number. There will be a showing this Saturday, the agent tells him.

He counts the days until Saturday in his slow way of doing everything lately, then ducks his head into his work, pressing his forehead into the stretch of days between now and then.

When he sits at his drafting table in the mornings, he thinks about ways to design a room in which two people would be prevented from seeing each other. The problem is, while he could prevent two people from seeing each other by creating various obstructions—screens, walls, curtains—he could not prevent either person from looking for the other. And it's the looking he wants to prevent through the arrangement of surfaces. But how to overcome this difference between seeing and looking eludes him like water does a convex surface.

He makes several sketches of a room divided by walls, waterfalls, and other obstructions, then realizes he's drawn these sketches on drafts of his client's house, setting himself back a week's worth of work, because now he will have to redraft the work he's done for his client, who is difficult enough as it is, and who will not tolerate falling water in his kitchen.

On Saturday he awakens through a dream: he is holding the frame of a mirror and encouraging a fox to leap through the mirror's frame as if it were a hoop. The fox refuses. Slowly he wakes to the day's gray morning.

He takes his time making coffee and puttering over the drawings on his drafting table. It's a dull project for a demanding client who has rejected his earlier two drafts. He understands that his boredom with this job is the boredom he feels for his work in general; for maybe a year now he cannot elaborate on a structure in his mind the way he used to, seeing everything clearly, then confidently mapping his vision onto paper. Now he gropes his way slowly across surfaces, moving his thoughts through a dull gray peace like dense fog that protects him from sharp sounds and surprises. He finds his clothes in this fog and puts them on. They're wrinkled. Then feels that he has put his sweater on backwards and reverses his earlier action.

His life has become this fog, this action/reverse action, and in it, he is aware of the feeling when he goes down or climbs up the stairs to his apartment as a feeling that exists only in relation to, and because of, the feeling he'd had moving up or down levels in his house, a feeling he'd shared with his wife—of being flung with some force away from a shared momentary center. Even this memory is dependent on and shared with her. He doesn't want to know how many such dependencies rule the present moment's sensations; he senses there are many.

By the time he is in his car driving toward the house, he is on time for his appointment with the agent, who on the phone mentioned that the owner might be around to help with the showing. She added, in reference to the house, You'll be pleased, I think, by the renovations. The owner has gone to a lot of effort.

In one draft, when he was still trying to work out the structure, he drew a long hallway in a figure-eight that passed through a central room or chamber, so that from above, the structure resembled a winged creature, a butterfly or an airplane. Passing through the central chamber, one could ascend or descend to the upper and lower levels by switching, via a ramp, to the top or underside of the hallway. This way, two people could be standing on two sides of the same geometric point without being aware of the other's presence, in a manner similar to the way two people may cross monkey bars, one person walking across, the other clinging to the bars, only in the hallway, each person would sense their feet were on the floor. He then complicated the structure by adding a second looping hallway, which created third and fourth wings perpendicular to the other two, one rising above ground, the other extending some distance below. But then the central chamber had to accommodate both lateral and vertical changes in direction, and this proved too complicated: if two people attempted to change direction in the central chamber at the same moment, one trying to move from a lateral wing to a vertical wing, and the other trying to move from the same vertical wing to the occupied lateral wing, there would be a painful collision that would surely cause both to become disillusioned with the structure's ability to accommodate more than one person at a time. Even if two people were to transition from one lateral wing to the other, the ramps accessing the third and fourth wings would simply put too much demand on the central chamber, and there could be a collision. And even without the third and fourth wings, if he went back to his original plan of two wings navigable by the Mobius hallway, he could see how there would be the danger of collision in the central chamber if both attempted to change position at the same time.

In the final version of the house, the one he built and lived in with his wife, there was no chance of a collision: he could pass through all of the levels as if in a dream, without having to attend to the effort of climbing or descending, and without sharp corners or stairs where, in a narrow space, he might have to confront someone face-to-face going the opposite direction.

But though his life became that dream-fog, now he is aware of the feeling when he goes down or climbs up the stairs to his apartment as a feeling that exists only in relation to, and because of, the feeling he'd had moving up or down levels in his house, a feeling which he'd shared with his wife—of being flung with some force away from a shared momentary center. These dependencies of feelings, one feeling seeming to arise out of the memory of a past feeling, build in his imagining a recursive structure, extending back to a first experience from which all others must arise—his birth, or could they extend back further? To some moment of movement shared with his mother, the experience of her voice from within...He realizes that he is driving and has no idea where he is.

He arrives twenty minutes late. The agent meets him in the driveway as he's preparing (sitting staring) to open the car door. The agent is his mother. She is smiling. He opens the door and says hello. She greets him politely, in the way he watched her greet strangers when he was a boy—with a smile that contracts the downturned tired lines around her eyes, pulls them inward toward the momentary centers of her pupils, holds them, and then releases them to the periphery of her face. She doesn't recognize him the way he does her.

You must be my one o'clock, she says, Mister...

He looks at his watch and says, Mr. Gray.

Yes, she says, Sorry, I'm terrible with names.

I have the same problem, he says, thinking, I get it from you. Then sees this woman who looks like his dead mother turn away from him to point up the driveway to the house.

The owner, Gary, is here, she says.

Great, he says, and does the smile that's a horizontal line suddenly tugged upward at both ends, then released to dangle.

She says, Please, follow me.

For maybe a year now he cannot elaborate on a structure in his mind the way he used to, seeing everything clearly, then confidently mapping his vision onto paper. Now he gropes his way slowly across sur-faces, moving his thoughts through a dull gray peace like dense fog that protects him from sharp sounds and surprises. The fog is an odd structure, made up of more twists, obstructions, and complications than most of its kind.

The photograph of the house in the ad showed only the entry and a fraction of the surrounding structure, so as he walks behind the agent up the driveway, he considers the renovations, what they might be, since the photograph revealed nothing.

Oh, hey, hi, I'm Gary. Could you help me for a sec?

Gary leans into the trunk of his car and pulls out a framed mirror. Could you carry this into the house? Gary passes him the mirror.

Sure, he says, unsurprised to be made use of by Gary, who he supposes has been living in his house, possibly with his ex-wife, changing what he'd worked to build.

Gary closes the trunk and turns toward him holding a framed mirror identical to the one in his own hands. Sorry, Gary says, To make you work, you don't even live here yet!

Then he remembers the mirror in his dream, the recalcitrant fox. To show himself there's really a mirror in the frame, he holds the frame away from his body and knees its center. He hears the glass break and feels a sharp pain in his knee.

The hell? says Gary.

Sorry, he says, I. I tripped.

You're bleeding, shit, here—

Mr. Gray watches as blood appears on his pant leg. Gary sets his mirror in the grass to the side of the driveway, takes the shattered mirror from Mr. Gray's hands, and stacks it atop the other.

Follow me, says Gary.

He limps slowly across the remaining driveway, moving his thoughts through a dull gray peace like dense fog that protects him from sharp sounds and surprises. He looks at what he can see of the house from the entry but doesn't yet notice the changes.

Oh, says the agent, who is standing in the entry when he and Gary pass through. You're bleeding, she says, and watches the blood stain change shape as it saturates his pant leg, the blood an affirmation that he is, in fact, alive.

God, says the agent, I'm tired. This house, something about it just tires me out. Bigger than it looks! I feel like I've walked all day by the time I finish showing it. Would you like a cup of tea before we get started?

His leg still bleeding in two distinct rivulets running down his shin from knee to ankle, he says, Sure.

Please, follow me.

He follows the agent along the familiar route from entry to kitchen, having lost track of Gary, whose voice he hears somewhere in the house.

In the final version of the house, the one he built and lived in with his wife, there was no chance of a collision: he could pass through all of the levels as if in a dream, without having to attend to the effort of climbing or descending, and without sharp corners or stairs where, in a narrow space, he might have to confront someone face-to-face going the opposite direction

How many people live here, he asks the agent.

Gary said just he and his wife. Their kids are grown, I guess, or they don't have kids, I don't remember which.

He feels again the strangeness of ascending what is in fact a flat surface, feels it most of all in his stomach, the feeling of taking a turn in a car at a high speed, when the body wants to continue traveling forward but the walls of the car force the body to travel in a different direction.

He brakes hard to avoid hitting a woman crossing the intersection though his light is green. He comes within inches of her and the car lurches, stops, and the motion throws his body in a different direction. The feeling of being flung with some force localizes in his knee, which has jammed under the dash. In his confusion he sees the woman look at him through the windshield, she's pale, as if about to faint, and then she does faint, flinging up her arms as she slouches to the pavement. Shit. He puts the car in park and gets out hoping nobody else has seen her drop. The pain in his knee is now of something embedded close to bone. He realizes he will be late to his appointment with the agent and wonders if he should call her now to let her know or after he has bent over the woman to make sure she's still breathing.

Here, says the agent, holding out a mug of tea, Earl gray.

Through a dull gray peace like dense fog that protects him from sharp sounds and surprises he reaches toward the agent and takes the mug by its handle. Thanks, he says.

Well, I suppose we should get on with the tour. The agent smiles and the lines of her face again match those of his dead mother's.

Are you okay, he asks, bending over the woman, who he sees is not dead because her eyes are blinking and her lips mumbling. Good, he says, Okay, can you hear me?

Sure, he says, After you. Holding the mug of steaming tea while following the agent he wonders if he will be able to manage what seems a difficult feat of balance with his knee feeling like a shard of glass is embedded in it.

The woman nods but says nothing.

You're bleeding, shit, here, he says, dabbing at a gash in her head. I'm going to call an ambulance. After the thirtieth or fortieth ring, the ring tone becomes not a sound but a series of pauses between affirmations that he is, in fact, alive. During those pauses weeks might go by, months, a year, his skin becoming flakier, his arms fleshier, his bathroom moldy, his dishes congealed, bruises he can't explain appearing on his body, then fading to greenish, then fading to flesh, then flaking off, accumulating in corners, his bodily flesh renewing itself despite his inner disintegration.

Leaving the kitchen, we come first to the dining room, says the agent. The remarkable thing about this house is, well, I'm not sure how to explain it. It's the strangest house I think I've ever...maybe it's just me, but after I walk through it, I feel like I've walked miles without getting anywhere.

He isn't sure how much time passes until the ambulance arrives. Could be an hour, could be ten minutes. He kneels on the pavement between the front of his car and the woman, keeping a hand on her body and listening to the sounds his engine makes as it's cooling. Then he listens at her lips.

He continues to hear Gary's voice talking in another part of the house, he isn't sure which. For maybe a year now he cannot elaborate on a structure in his mind the way he used to, seeing everything clearly, then confidently mapping his vision onto paper. He tries to remember the layout of the house as he designed it, the dependencies among spaces, one space arising out of the memory of the space just passed through, building in his imagining a recursive structure. It's an odd structure, made up of twists, obstructions, and complications:

The staircase leads from the living room to the master bedroom, says the agent. It's one of Gary's renovations.

The staircase spirals in such tight circles it's difficult to tell whether it will lead him up or down. Even after the first several stairs, he isn't sure in which direction he's going. Gary's voice sounds farther away, but another voice sounds nearer. It's a woman's voice, and she's saying something about

Sorry, the woman says, sitting up from the pavement. I didn't see you coming. You look so familiar, it's weird. Have I met you before? No, I don't think, he says. The woman stands. Well, she says, Good to meet you, and laughs, lightly touching the gash on the back of her head.

He sees the ambulance arrive in his rearview as he's driving away. Two EMTs in blue jumpsuits stand in the intersection with their hands in their pockets, and they're searching for the body, turning in slow circles, each turning in the opposite direction of the other, so that they look like spools reeling in the road behind him.

You see what I mean about walking all day and not getting anywhere? the agent says, turning to look back at him as they continue taking stairs quickly, the woman's voice becoming much louder as they must be nearing the master bedroom. He, forgetful lately about hygiene, pats his hair down, thinking about the possibility of seeing his ex-wife again after all these years. Imagining an empty white room, his little learned trick to hold a thought so it won't elude him, he holds the image of her surprised face at the center of the room, just a hovering surprised face, and cannot help but look down and see a fat belly connected to his ex-wife's face, Gary.

Having thought he was ascending through many levels, further and further from the entry, he ends right back at the entry. He isn't sure how much time has passed, could be an hour, could be ten minutes.

You must be my one o'clock, Mister...

He looks at his watch and says, Mr. Gray.

Yes, she says, Sorry, I'm terrible with names.

The glare of the sun is bright off a small pond in the spot where he recalls earlier Gary stacked two mirrors. Gary sits beside the pond, one leg hung down into the gray water, the voice of a woman rising out of the pond.

Would you like a cup of tea before we get started?

Great, he says, and does the smile that's a horizontal line suddenly tugged upward at both ends, then released to dangle. Then sees this woman who looks like his dead mother turn away from him. The pain is now of something embedded close to bone.

Please, follow me.

CONTRIBUTORS

DANIELLE ADAIR is an artist and writer born in northern Michigan and currently based in Los Angeles. She is the author of *From JBAD: Lessons Learned* (Les Figues Press, 2009) a "field guide" based on her time as a media embed with US Forces in Afghanistan. Select writing has also appeared in *Valeveil, [out of nothing], Poetry Sz, GLARE Quarterly,* and *Afterall Online,* and her video-performance work has screened internationally. Danielle is the recipient of the 2010 California Community Foundation Fellowship, and more about her work can be found at www.danielleadair.com and www. first-assignment.com.

ANGI BECKER STEVENS's stories have appeared in such places as *Barrelhouse, The Collagist, Pank, SmokeLong Quarterly, Storyglossia, Necessary Fiction, Monkeybicycle, Wigleaf,* and *The Best of the Web 2010.* She lives with her family in Michigan.

MATT BELL is the author of *How They Were*

Found, a collection of fiction from Keyhole Press. His stories have been anthologized in *Best American Mystery Stories 2010* and *Best American Fantasy 2.* He is also the editor of *The Collagist* and can be found online at www.mdbell.com.

KRISTINA BORN is 23, 5'2", 105 lbs. She lives in Vancouver, B.C., and blogs at kristinaborn.blogspot. com. The novel excerpted here, *One Hour of Television,* was published by Year of the Liquidator in November, 2009.

RYAN CALL's stories appear in *Caketrain, Hobart, Lo-Ball, The Collagist, Mid-American Review, New York Tyrant, The Lifted Brow,* and elsewhere. He and his wife live in Houston.

JOSHUA COHEN's most recent novel is *Witz.* A new edition of his first novel, *A Heaven of Others,* has just been released by Starcherone Books.

BETH COUTURE has work published or forthcoming in *Gargoyle, The Southeast Review, Drunken Boat,* and the *Dirty Fabulous Anthology* from Jaded Ibis, among others. She teaches composition at Bloomsburg University in Bloomsburg, PA.

IAN DAVISSON lives in Philadelphia in the ritziest neighborhood, where he eats the fanciest food and canoodles with the upper-classiest ladies. He works as a cabana boy at the Lombard Swim Club in Rittenhouse Square, and is considering 99 weeks of unemployment checks. He's been published online at *Lamination Colony* and other places, and pieces from his collaboration with Ryan Downey can be seen on *Lamination Colony*. He was nominated for a Pushcart. He comes from Atlanta and attributes his creative impulse to the music and personalities of Outkast and the Three 6 Mafia.

ZACH DODSON's hybrid typo/graphic novel, *boring boring boring boring boring boring boring*, came out in 2008 under the nom de plume Zach Plague. He has launched such experiments as Featherproof Books, Bleached Whale Design, and *The Show N' Tell Show*. His writing has appeared in *Monsters & Dust, ACM, Lamination Colony*, and *Proximity Magazine*. He is currently working on a sci-fi/historical southwestern adventure romance about bats.

RYAN DOWNEY has taken degrees in comparative literature and creative writing from the University of Georgia and the University of Notre Dame respectively. He teaches at Malcolm X College, Wright College, St. Augustine College, and in the Chicago Public Schools for the Poetry Center of Chicago. His hybrid-text, *MAW MAW*, has recently been named as a semi-finalist for the 2011 Madeline P. Plonsker Emerging Writer's Residency Prize, and two chapbooks, *Poems From a News*

Ticker (Scantily Clad Press, 2009) and *This is the Fall Line* (mud luscious press, 2010), can be found with some basic Googling. He lives in Chicago with his historian wife, Allison Bertke Downey, and his growing clan of orange cats.

JACLYN DWYER earned an MFA from the University of Notre Dame, where she received the Sparks Fellowship. Her work can be seen in a number of literary magazines including *The Cortland Review, Monkeybicycle*, and *3am magazine*. She is currently enrolled in Florida State's PhD program in Creative Writing.

ANDREW FARKAS's *Self-Titled Debut* won the Subito Press Book Competition and was published in December 2008. His work has appeared in *The Cincinnati Review, Copper Nickel, Artifice Magazine, Pank, The Brooklyn Rail,* and other journals. He is from Akron, Ohio, but currently lives in Chicago.

ELISA GABBERT is the poetry editor of *Absent* and the author of *The French Exit* (Birds, LLC) and *Thanks for Sending the Engine* (Kitchen Press). Her poems have appeared in *Colorado Review, Denver Quarterly, The Laurel Review, Pleiades, Salt Hill,* and *Sentence,* among other journals, and her nonfiction has appeared in *Mantis, Open Letters Monthly,* and *The Monkey & The Wrench: Essays into Contemporary Poetics.* She currently lives in Boston, works at a software startup, and blogs at The French Exit (thefrenchexit.

blogspot.com).

RACHEL B. GLASER lives in Northampton, MA with the writer John Maradik. She grew up in New Jersey, and attended Rhode Island School of Design and Umass-Amherst. She appreciates NBA culture, hand drawn animation, Queen, Pavement, and MS Paint. Her story "Infections" is included in her first book "Pee On Water," which was recently published by Publishing Genius Press. Read more of her work at rachelbglaser. blogspot.com or talk to her at bassethoundfound@ gmail.com.

ADAM GOOD is an interdisciplinary artist living in Pittsboro, NC. His performance lectures, interactive experiences, writings, and installations utilize methods of appropriation, remixing, participation, and improvisation. Recent work includes *The Lab for Remixed Knowledge* (at Washington Project for the Arts), *One Hour Photo* (at the Katzen Arts Center), and *Isle Atollish* (a collaboration with Lauren Bender, at Transmodern). His work can be viewed on his website, www.therealadamgood. com.

DEVIN GRIBBONS is currently an MFA student at the University of Alabama and is considered by many to be a song and dance man. His self-esteem depends heavily upon your adoration. He will be graduating soon.

EVELYN HAMPTON lives in Providence. Her website is Lispservice.com.

SHANE JONES lives in upstate New York and blogs at ivomiticecubessowhat.com. He's the author of *Light Boxes* (PGP 2009, Penguin 2010). A new novel, *Daniel Fights a Hurricane* is scheduled to be published by Penguin in early 2012. Shane can be reached at Sejones85@gmail.com.

SEAN KILPATRICK is in the MA program at EMU, published in *Columbia Poetry Review, Tarpaulin Sky, Caketrain, LIT, Fence, No Colony, Dzanc Best of the Web 2010*, and a first book, *fuckscapes*, forthcoming with Blue Square Press.

ANDREA KNEELAND has no plans for the future. Her work has appeared or is forthcoming in a number of journals, including *Quick Fiction, Weird Tales, Hobart, Caketrain, American Letters & Commentary, 580 Split, Night Train, elimae, DIAMGRAM, alice blue review, Whiskey Island, Storyglossia, The Binnacle, Dogzplot,* and *Lamination Colony*. Her first collection of flash fiction, *Damage Control*, is forthcoming from Paper Hero Press as a part of the *Fox Force 5* chapbook collective.

CHRISTINA KLOESS is currently a Chicago-based writer. She has twice won the Indiana State Project XL competition in the writing category, and received the Friends of American Writers scholarship in 2009. She has been published in *Mythic Circles* journal and in the Chicago Tribune. Christina is pursuing her MFA in fiction writing at Roosevelt University.

REBECCA JEAN KRAFT's written and visual material has been used on the *Late Show with David Letterman*, she writes jokes professionally, and she holds a current Guinness World Record, "The Most Shrimp Eaten Out Of A Human Mouth By A Duck." Her work can be found in *Word Riot, The Pedestal Magazine,* and *The Potomac,* among others.

By choice, MICHAEL J. LEE awaits his summons in New Orleans, Louisiana. A frequent contributor to *Conjunctions*, his debut story collection, *Something in My Eye*, is forthcoming from Sarabande Books.

CONOR ROBIN MADIGAN was born in Atlanta, Georgia in 1982. In January 2011, *Cut Up*, his first novel, will be published by The Republic of Letters Books, with illustrations.

MEGAN MILKS co-edits *Mildred Pierce Zine* and co-hosts Uncalled-for Readings Chicago. Her work has been anthologized in *The &NOW Awards, Wreckage of Reason*, and *Fist of the Spider Woman: Tales of Fear and Queer Desire*. Her stories can also be found in *Western Humanities Review, Everyday Genius, Mon-*

sters and Dust, and *The Wild,* among other journals. "Slug" has been adapted for performance on Montreal-based CKUT's *Audio Smut* radio show; "Tomato Heart" has been adapted for a performance piece by Cathy Nicoli. "Kill Marguerite" is available as a chapbook through Another New Calligraphy Press.

BRIAN OLIU is originally from New Jersey and currently lives in Tuscaloosa, Alabama. His work has been published in *Hotel Amerika, New Ohio Review, Brevity, DIAGRAM, Sonora Review, Ninth Letter,* and others. This is an automated message.

KATHLEEN ROONEY is a founding editor of Rose Metal Press, and the author, most recently, of the essay collection *For You, For You I Am Trilling These Songs* (Counterpoint, 2010). Her poetry collection, *Oneiromance: an epithalamion,* won the 2007 Gatewood Prize from the feminist publisher Switchback Books, and her collaborative collection, *That Tiny Insane Voluptuousness,* was published by Otoliths in 2008.

JOANNA RUOCCO co-edits *Birkensnake,* a fiction journal. She is the author of the novel *The Mothering Coven* (Ellipsis Press) and the short story collection *Man's Companions* (Tarpaulin Sky Press). Her chapbook of prose fragments, *A Compendium of Domestic Incidents,* is forthcoming from Noemi Press.

TODD SEABROOK is an MFA student at the University of Colorado and has had stories published in *New Ohio Review, Squid Quarterly,* and *Quiddity.*

MICHAEL STEWART was the 2010 Rhode Island Council for the Arts Fellow in both fiction and poetry. His work has appeared in a variety of journals and anthologies including *Conjunctions, Denver Quarterly,* and *American Letters & Commentary.* In early 2011 his novel(la) *The Hieroglyphics* will be out with mud luscious press. Currently, he lectures about all sorts of things at Brown University. If you're interested, you can find more of his work at: strangesympathies. com.

JAMES YEH (b. 1982) is a writer, editor, and occasional DJ. His stories, nonfiction, and interviews have appeared in *PEN America, Vice, The Rumpus,* and elsewhere. He is a founding editor of *Gigantic* and lives in Brooklyn, NY.

MIKE YOUNG is the author of *We Are All Good If They Try Hard Enough,* a poetry collection, and *Look! Look! Feathers,* a story collection. He co-edits *NOÖ Journal,* runs Magic Helicopter Press, and writes for HTMLGIANT. Find him online at mikeayoung.blogspot. com.

EDITORS

BLAKE BUTLER lives in Atlanta and is Editor of the literature blog *HTMLGIANT* and the journals *Lamination Colony* and, with Ken Bauman, *No Colony*. He is the author of three books, the novella, *Ever* (Calamari Press, 2009), the novel-in-stories, *Scorch Atlas* (Featherproof Books, 2009), and the recently released novel, *There Is No Year* (Harper Perennial, 2011). He has published more than one hundred stories in magazine and journals, both online and in print.

LILY HOANG was born in San Antonio, Texas, to parents who had fled Vietnam in 1975. Her first book, *Parabola* (2008), won the Chiasmus Press Un-Doing the Novel Contest. She is also the author of the novels *Changing* (Fairy Tale Review Press, 2008), which received a PEN Beyond Margins Award, and *The Evolutionary Revolution* (Les Figues Press, 2010), and *Unfinished* (2011), a collection of stories begun by other contemporary authors. She is currently an Assistant Professor of English at New Mexico State University.

Also available from Starcherone Books

Kenneth Bernard, *The Man in the Stretcher: previously uncollected stories*
Donald Breckenridge, *You Are Here*
Joshua Cohen, *A Heaven of Others*
Peter Conners, ed., *PP/FF: An Anthology*
Jeffrey DeShell, *Peter: An (A)Historical Romance*
Nicolette deCsipkay, *Black Umbrella Stories*, illustrated by Francesca deCsipkay
Raymond Federman, *My Body in Nine Parts*, with photographs by Steve Murez
Raymond Federman, *Shhh: The Story of a Childhood*
Raymond Federman, *The Voice in the Closet*
Raymond Federman and **George Chambers**, *The Twilight of the Bums*, with cartoon accompaniment by T. Motley
Sara Greenslit, *The Blue of Her Body*
Johannes Göransson, *Dear Ra: A Story in Flinches*
Joshua Harmon, *Quinnehtukqut*
Harold Jaffe, *Beyond the Techno-Cave: A Guerrilla Writer's Guide to Post-Millennial Culture*
Stacey Levine, *The Girl with Brown Fur: stories & tales*
Janet Mitchell, *The Creepy Girl and other stories*
Alissa Nutting, *Unclean Jobs for Women and Girls*
Aimee Parkison, *Woman with Dark Horses: Stories*
Ted Pelton, *Endorsed by Jack Chapeau 2 an even greater extent*
Thaddeus Rutkowski, *Haywire*
Leslie Scalapino, *Floats Horse-Floats or Horse-Flows*
Nina Shope, *Hangings: Three Novellas*

Starcherone Books, Inc., is a 501(c)(3) non-profit whose mission is to stimulate public interest in works of innovative fiction. In addition to encouraging the growth of amateur and professional authors and their audiences, Starcherone seeks to educate the public in self-publishing and encourage the growth of other small presses. Visit us online at www.starcherone.com and the Starcherone Superfan Group on Facebook.

Starcherone Books is an independently operated imprint of Dzanc Books, distributed through Consortium Distribution and Small Press Distribution. We are a signatory to the Book Industry Treatise on Responsible Paper Use and use postconsumer recycled fiber paper in our books.

Starcherone Books, PO Box 303, Buffalo, NY 14201.